Out of

LEFT
FIELD

Out of

LEFT
FIELD

KRIS HUI LEE

sourcebooks
fire

Published by Sourcebooks Fire, an imprint of Sourcebooks, Inc.
P.O. Box 4410, Naperville, Illinois 60567-4410
(630) 961-3900
Fax: (630) 961-2168
sourcebooks.com

Library of Congress Cataloging-in-Publication Data

Names: Lee, Kris Hui, author.
Title: Out of left field / Kris Hui Lee.
Description: Naperville, Illinois : Sourcebooks Fire, [2018] | Summary: "Can
  Marnie pitch for the boy's baseball team and field an unexpected crush
  without striking out at the game...and in love?"-- Provided by publisher.
Identifiers: LCCN 2017051758 | (pbk. : alk. paper)
Subjects: | CYAC: Baseball--Fiction. | Friendship--Fiction. | Love--Fiction.
Classification: LCC PZ7.1.L4173 Out 2018 | DDC [Fic]--dc23 LC record
available at https://lccn.loc.gov/2017051758

Printed and bound in the United States of America.
VP 10 9 8 7 6 5 4 3 2 1

To BIFFLE,
who knew Marnie & Co. back when they were still
in junior high.

1

SEVENTEEN YEARS OF EXISTENCE HAVE TAUGHT
me many lessons—some relevant to survival, others not so
much—but one that I have come to fully understand is
that there are three kinds of idiocy.

The first is what I call Mundane Idiocy. This is the type
of idiocy that happens when you, say, walk into a dark room
thinking you can manage without the lights, and then you
stub your toe on a table. It happens to the best of us.

The second kind is Voluntary Idiocy. Sticking your
tongue to a frozen pole or prodding a beehive with a stick
or eating fourteen brownies in one sitting would fall under
this category. Discretion is advised.

And finally, the last level of idiocy has been achieved by
only one person, and his name is Cody Kinski.

Here I am, in the bleachers of my high school baseball field on a brisk May night—crickets chirping in the darkness beyond the bright stadium lights, the scent of french fries hitching a ride on the gentle breeze. I'm on the tips of my toes, waiting in anticipation like all my fellow game goers. Usually the excitement at high school baseball games never gets higher than the occasional collective gasp after a great hit followed by an anticlimactic defensive play, but our team is far from what you'd call usual. And this particular game is miles from being typical.

It's the bottom of the seventh. The last inning. There are two outs and two strikes. Kyle's on first. Cody's at bat. We're down five to four, and even though, to me, it feels like our chances of turning it around are borderline zero, everyone else seems to have an ounce of belief left in them.

The pitcher's given name is Santino Acardi, but in our neck of the woods, he is commonly known as Douche Face.

There are only two things you need to know about this olive-skinned, curly-haired, smarmy bastard: (1) no one on this planet knows how to wear a condescending, self-righteous smirk like he does, and (2) every time he and Cody get within two hundred feet of each other, the apocalypse seems imminent. I mean, they're two of the best pitchers in our entire region. They have both been playing on varsity since freshman year, on teams with a notorious rivalry. It's the kind of clash that's going to put an end to the world as we know it.

Basically every time Cody has been up at bat during this game, Santino has thrown at least one brushback pitch past Cody's face. It is only thanks to Cody's lightning-fast reflexes that he hasn't been knocked unconscious. Santino has been pulling this stunt since freshman year. He suffers from an oversize ego. Jock stuff—you know the deal.

Standing behind home plate, bat raised over his shoulder, eyes focused on Santino, Cody looks beyond prepared. He's ready for anything. And he should be, considering Santino's brushbacks are consistent. Parents, classmates, and residents from around the neighborhood cheer for Cody all across the home-team bleachers. Iron-Arm Kinski, they call him. He was first dubbed that when he was eight by his Little League coach. His killer fastball got him that name, but Cody is one hell of a hitter too. He's not a god, but sometimes he doesn't seem to be entirely human.

On the mound, Santino winds up his pitch. Every part of his body, from his long legs to his muscular arms, displays his power.

Then it comes. The ball launches out of Santino's hand at Major League speed.

Right toward Cody's head.

But he must not be as prepared as he seemed.

Does he move out of the way?

No.

He stands there like a moron, like there's *not* some sadist on the mound. It's only at the very last second that his left arm flies up to shield his head.

The ball smashes into Cody's left forearm. His bat clatters to the ground, and it's like everyone from here to the moon and beyond gasps. Cody clutches his arm to his chest as his face twists in pain. It's a look I recognize to mean *I've broken a bone, and I'm in some real fucking pain.*

Fire from the pits of hell radiate from the glare Cody shoots Santino, and if I were Santino, I'd want to jump on the next flight out of the country. All of Cody's fury and hatred—three years in the making—engulfs his face, his whole body. Cody has never been the kind of guy to be provoked by cheap shots, which I've learned in the eleven years I've known him, but right now, not even I can predict his next move.

But even though he might want to react, Cody doesn't get the opportunity. Jack Chizz, our coach, runs out to home plate as the ump calls, "Time!"

Joey, our guy on deck and Cody's best friend, follows Chizz. The three of them—Chizz, the ump, and

Joey—gather around Cody, blocking my view of what's happening.

Santino's cronies in the outfield crowd together too, but unlike those huddled around home plate, they seem unconcerned about what their overlord Santino has done. And Santino, for all the emotion he's showing, might as well be standing in line at a grocery store. I'm surprised he isn't shooting off fireworks and confetti of triumph over his good aim.

The buzzing energy is gone, and it's replaced by silent anticipation.

And then:

"WOOOO! WAY TO GO, CODY!"

This is Sara, who's standing next to me. To everyone else, it probably sounds like a cheer of encouragement. But Sara is no overzealous cheerleader.

She's teasing him.

"You're an asshole," I tell her, trying to keep a straight face.

Under the florescent lights, her normally tawny skin seems lighter. Her grin widens as she claps loudly. "Bringin' 'em to state!"

"Oh my gosh," I mutter, but I can't help but laugh a little. Sara, like me, has more than a decade of history with Cody, which entitles her to be a complete asshole to him in this very serious and stressful moment.

Cody, who has gotten some breathing room, takes off his batting helmet to reveal his disheveled dark brown hair. He then takes a moment out of the time-out to nonchalantly scratch his forehead with his middle finger in our direction. Those eleven years of friendship work in Cody's favor too—he gets a pass on being nice.

Cody drops his hand and listens intently to what Chizz is saying. At first, they both seem rather calm, given what's happened, but then Chizz says something else, and Cody goes ballistic. His eyes bulge in rage, and his uninjured arm flies in all directions. Cody points to first base. Chizz points a commanding finger toward the dugout.

"Don't be an idiot, Cody," I mutter. "Go to the hospital."

As if he can hear me, Cody kicks his bat to the side and stalks toward first. Chizz objects, but Cody shrugs him off. The interaction looks dramatic from here, which is so unlike Cody. He has always been a quiet, modest guy, but being on the field changes him. Out there, he's the confident jock everyone expects him to be.

Everyone cheers as Cody takes his base.

I wonder if they can see him wince in pain with every step. *Proud, stubborn bastard.*

As the game resumes, so does the crowd's excitement. They're exhilarated by Cody's perseverance (or, as I would call it, idiocy).

The count: two outs, zero strikes, with Kyle on second, Cody on first, and Joey at bat.

Tufts of Joey's blond hair stick out from under his batting helmet as he steps up to the plate and takes a few practice swings. This is a guy who walks into closed glass doors and trips on perfectly tied shoelaces, but I swear he has magic powers when he's on the field. He will move mountains to catch a foul ball and has been known to belt homers at the exact moment they're needed. You'd never know it though, because he can be a real baby sometimes. A few months ago, he was reduced to an inconsolable teary mess after he found out his ex-girlfriend is a lesbian. No one would have guessed at the time that the crying weenie he was then is our best hope for bringing in a miraculous run to tie up the game now.

On the mound, Santino winds up again. One of his trademarks is his sidearm pitching style. That's why he's one of the best; he's unique. I feel like a traitor, but I must admit that I admire his skill.

He throws the first pitch against Joey: foul tip. Strike one.

Second pitch: the ball and bat connect, and the crowd gasps. It's a foul over the first baseline. There's a collective sigh. Strike two.

The count: two outs, two strikes, five to four. The hopelessness settles in deeper.

On the third pitch, Joey smacks the ball with an echoing *clink!* and he runs. Screams of excitement follow him.

The ball soars toward the fence. It looks like it will be a home run between left and center field. Unfortunately, that's the kind of luck you can only dream about.

The ball hits the back fence and bounces onto the grass where two fielders race to snatch it up.

Kyle's past third, on his way to home, and Cody's passing second.

The ball is traveling from the outfield to shortstop.

Kyle's foot lands on home plate. It's now five to five.

Cody's foot hits third.

From the dugout, Chizz shouts at Cody to stop where he is.

The ball is at the shortstop.

And Cody's going home.

"Idiot!" Sara and I both shout.

But it's no use. The ball and Cody race toward home.

The throw to the catcher is off by a foot. He steps away. Cody dives, headfirst, arms outstretched.

He collides with home plate and becomes buried under a plume of sand and the catcher.

"Safe!" the ump shouts. "Safe!"

The shouting and cheering intensify as our team hops over the dugout wall and dog piles Joey, who brought in the runs. Santino and his team look like they're about to commit fifteen different types of manslaughter.

And there, still on the ground in the fetal position clutching his arm, ladies and gentlemen, is the third and final category of idiocy: Cody Kinski.

2

I HAVEN'T BEEN IN THE CORRINGTON FIELD DUGOUTS since freshman year, back when I was on the softball team. It feels familiar, walking across the infield, past the pitcher's mound, the sand dusting my shoes. But it also feels unfamiliar, like it might have been a dream. Normally, unauthorized personnel are not allowed on the field or in the dugouts, but seeing as everyone is too busy freaking out about the team's win, no one notices us. And even if someone *did*, Sara and I would still march across the infield to see our injured, moronic friend.

On our way to the dugout, we catch snippets of conversations:

"I can't *believe* Cody got injured!"

"Who's going to pitch at sectionals now?"

"Santino will be watching his back for the rest of his life."

"Did you see Cody flip off Sara Fox after he got hit?"

"Does Cody have a girlfriend?"

"He's *so* hot."

"Now we'll never make it to state, let alone the semifinals."

The same thoughts churn in my mind too. Well, the ones pertaining to baseball, not Cody's relationship status. It was pretty much guaranteed that our team has a spot in the state finals. We've got one of the best high school coaches in the nation, a killer pitcher, some of the biggest hitters in the region, and four guys who were on the team three years ago when they won the state title.

At least going to state *was* guaranteed until about ten minutes ago when Cody got nailed in the arm.

I mean, sure, we've got relief pitchers, but none who can even begin to match Cody's talent. This means that sectionals, which used to be an easy step to the top, is now as much as a mountain to climb as the semifinals and the state game.

In our team's dugout, the guys are huddled in a tight bunch shouting over one another. Chizz is nowhere to be found. Neither is Cody. I'm so focused on finding out how Cody is that I don't even see the Willow Heights team approaching until they cut right in front of me and Sara on their way to the buses.

Sara pulls my arm so I don't walk right into their paths. They death march past us, so close we can smell their sweat. In the presence of their tall, looming figures, I forget all about Cody. Instead, the scathing voice in my head says, *Screw you and you and you and you*, and I zero in on Santino and think, *Especially you, asshole.* But I keep my mouth shut because I know eighteen guys against me and Sara are not good odds.

But then this one really short guy looks over at us—or, more precisely, at Sara—and then he looks down to Sara's tank top and then down her long, tan legs, and then at her oblivious face.

I'm no stranger to assholes checking out Sara. Her Filipino and Hispanic parents gave her a melting-pot look that is difficult to walk past without noticing. She attracts guys and girls (and conveniently for her, she is attracted *to* guys and girls). Even the dogs at her mom's shelter seem to like her more than they like other people.

I give him the evil eye, but he doesn't notice. He nudges his friend, glances back at Sara, and then makes an extremely vulgar gesture involving his finger going through a hole he's made with his other hand.

When I was younger, I used to pick fights all the time.

I'd find all sorts of reasons to have a go at someone. It's still a struggle to restrain myself, even though I'm supposedly more mature. But there's no way in hell this guy is taking another step. Not without hearing a word from me first.

I catch his name on the back of his jacket and call, "Hey, Jonings!"

He and a couple of friends slow their walks, trying to figure out who's calling.

"What's it like to be the same height as your bat?" I say. "Go back to the Shire!"

Sara snaps her head toward me, her eyes wide in confusion and amusement. "Nice," she says, "but kind of uncalled for?"

"Trust me. It wasn't," I say as Jonings marches over.

It's only when my gaze meets Jonings's glare that I realize I've probably made a very big mistake. *Good job, Marnie. Why the hell do you always have to open your big mouth?*

I can't let him think he can scare me with those clenched fists and demonic eyes.

"What did you say?" he questions, two of his teammates flanking him. Up close, the top of his head hardly reaches my chin, which makes him slightly less intimidating.

"What?" I say. "Did Bilbo Baggins forget to teach you how to not be a dick wad?"

I mentally pat myself on the back. My arsenal of insults never ceases to amaze me.

But in a matter of seconds, I go from congratulating myself to anticipating a punch in the gut. I'm about to pull Sara in front of me, because she's the one with the black belt in karate, when, seemingly out of nowhere, Santino Acardi yanks Jonings away from behind.

"Leave it, Alan," he says. He glares at me, dragging Jonings to where the rest of their team is loading onto the buses.

Sara and I stare silently after them. She's probably wondering what the hell is wrong with me, and I'm wondering the same thing.

"What the hell was that?"

Sara and I both turn, and I bump into Cody.

"A Lord of the Rings insult?" he says to me. "Really?"

I take in his tousled brown hair, his sand-covered red-and-black uniform, and the careful way he carries his very swollen left wrist. It's the semigrin on his face that throws me off. Here he is, nailed with a ninety-mile-per-hour pitch, and he sounds like it's any other day.

Then Joey appears, jumping Sara from behind, making her shout and punch him in the chest.

"So you picking fights again?" Joey asks me as he picks a fight with Sara, putting her in a loose headlock. She shoves him off, and Joey shakes his head at me. "It's like you're *looking* for an ass whooping."

"I could've handled it," I say.

"You know he only left you alone because he saw me and Joey coming," Cody adds, knowing as much as I do that I could not have handled it. "Who'd be scared by this scrawny thing anyway?" he says, flipping my long auburn hair in my face.

I push his hand away, about to remind him that his six-foot frame only has three inches on mine, but then I realize that he's still *here* and not where he should be, which is at a hospital. "Don't you have an injury to take care of or something?" I ask him.

In response, Cody glances back to the dugout, where Chizz and Mr. Kinski are in deep conversation, most likely about what to do with Cody. Since last summer, Cody's been on track to play ball in college. He went to a bunch of baseball camps and has spent a lot of time working with professional pitching coaches. This postseason was supposed to prove his worth to the scouts. His dad and Chizz have been working relentlessly to get him scholarships and attract the eyes of college coaches.

"Hey, Marnie," Sara says. "Maybe you should take Cody's place. Chizz would love that." She says this with a straight face, but she must be joking. No way in hell Chizz—not to mention the guys—would let me on the team.

Case in point: "Hell, no," Joey says. "Over my dead body."

"Gladly," Sara says, grinning. She starts fake-boxing him, and he fake-boxes back. Cody and I exchange the same look we always do when Sara and Joey, well, do this. We don't call it flirting because that ship sunk sometime last year. No one knows what actually happened between them, but we do know this: (1) We don't talk about it. (2) They didn't speak to—or even look at—each other for almost six months after it happened. (3) Even now, sometimes it gets weird between them, and we don't know why, so basically… (4) Hooking up with someone you've known for eleven years is a Bad Idea™.

Sara stops play-punching Joey in the gut and points over my shoulder. "Here he comes. Let's ask him."

Before any of us can object, Sara calls, "Hey, Chizz!" She waves him over to us.

Chizz and Mr. Kinski approach, both looking tired and defeated, despite the regional game win. Mr. Kinski looks like Cody—tall with messy, dark hair and pin-straight posture—only he has a goatee. He and I are on pretty good terms, considering all the trouble I've gotten Cody into. It's Chizz that I've got to look out for. He has some sort of vendetta against me, and I've got no idea why. I've had him as my gym teacher two years in a row, and I have been nothing but a model student. I always get the fastest mile times, always participate, always help put the equipment away when everyone else rushes to the locker rooms…

Okay, so *maybe* I clobbered Joey in the head with a tennis racket once. I swear it was an accident. And *maybe* I can be *slightly* aggressive and mouth off at times. But I really am an ideal student.

"So, Chizz," Sara says. "What do you think about letting Marnie on the mound for postseason, eh?"

"I think it's time for you to go home," Chizz says with a sigh, clearly in no mood for dealing with the four of us.

I play along with Sara. "Aw, come on, Chizz. We all know I'm a better pitcher than Cody."

"Ha!" Joey shouts. "You wish. You've got nothing on my boy."

"Well, since *your boy* is now an invalid, who's gonna pitch for you at the sandlot tomorrow?" I taunt. "Right. Me. So *shh*."

Chizz shakes his head and starts walking away. Normally, he'd at least *try* and be an authoritative figure when we start acting like twelve-year-olds, but I guess the burden of losing his star pitcher is too much for him.

"Come on, Cody," Mr. Kinski says, offering to take his duffel bag. "We have to get you to the hospital."

It's only then that Cody's carefree demeanor falters. His body stiffens, and the amused grin on his face—put there by Sara, Joey, and me bickering—falls as the crinkles around his eyes disappear. That's how it is with Cody. He's the quiet one. You can't wait for him to say what he's thinking or feeling. You have to watch his face or the way he walks or stands or looks at his surroundings. It took me almost ten years to figure out how to read him, but I've got it down now.

In the next moment, his look of dread is replaced by a crooked grin. Before following his dad to the car, he says to me, "I suppose telling you not to pick fights won't do any good, so try not to get your ass kicked while I'm not here to defend you."

I know he's joking around to cover his disappointment over his injury, and because it's easier to play along than to be serious, I go, "I told you. I could've handled it."

"Whatever you say." He flips my hair in my face again, even though he knows I hate it when he does that.

I slap his hand away. "Hey, when you're at the hospital, tell the doctor to surgically remove the ass hat on your head."

"I appreciate your concern," he says with a grin, taking a few steps back.

I blow him a kiss as he starts following his dad to their car. To anyone else, it might seem endearing, perhaps even romantic, but Cody has known me a long time and understands that any kiss I blow his way is only out of irony. He returns my kiss with his middle finger. So it goes in our relationship.

When I turn around, I find Sara and Joey staring at me, eyebrows raised, condescending smirks on their faces.

"What?"

At the same time, they both go, "Nothing." Joey brushes some residual sand off his uniform and picks up his gym bag. "Sandlot tomorrow," he reminds us both. "Be late, and I'll bury you alive." He waves down a couple of other guys from the team and jogs over to them.

Sara and I head off on our own. Even though we've both got our licenses, we still like to walk between our houses and to school. On a night like this, there's no reason to contribute to air pollution.

Much like I don't ask her what the hell happened between her and Joey, she doesn't try playing cupid with me. Recently Sara has decided that Cody likes me, and even more ludicrously, that I return those feelings. First of all, Cody would rather have his eyes clawed out by rabid werewolves than like me. And second of all, I would not only rather have my eyes clawed out by rabid werewolves, I would also rather be stung to death by rabid jellyfish. There is only one rule for having a ten-year friendship with someone: *like*-liking is strictly prohibited. *Liking* will ruin a friendship because *liking* always leads to heartache. Exhibit A: Joey and Sara.

Sara doesn't have to say anything for me to know what she's thinking. The look she and Joey exchanged was enough for me to read between the lines. Instead of forcing her to spit it out, I ignore the cupid vibes she's emitting and stare out at the field.

The lights are still on, bathing the vacant infield in a fluorescent glow. I imagine Santino on the mound, the sheer power behind his windup, and the ninety-mile-per-hour pitch that no doubt amazed the college scouts in the bleachers.

For a moment, I picture myself out there on the mound. I haven't played competitively since freshman year when I was on the varsity softball team. Back then, I used to imagine being the star pitcher of the team. Sometimes I liked to think of Cody and me as king and queen of the pitcher's mound—him in baseball, me in softball. And who knows, maybe we would have reigned. But then I quit. The pressure got to be too much. I don't like to talk about it. So Cody's the last one standing, as he should be, considering he would never let his team down the way I did.

Sure, when Sara jokingly suggested I take Cody's place, I had a brief moment of *Eureka!* Like, *Yeah, let me do it.*

But the thought of stepping foot on that field is even more ridiculous than the thought of Cody liking me. More ridiculous than the thought of me liking Cody.

In short, me playing on the guys' team would no doubt fall under a brand-new category of idiocy.

3

I'M SURE THERE WAS A TIME BEFORE THE
sandlot, before Cody and Joey and Sara, before our
weekend pickup games at the park, before I was a fight-
picking, loudmouthed, baseball-obsessed jock, but hell if I
can remember it. It's as if some other me in some alternate
reality lived through those five years. But not *this* me.

Almost like clockwork, I wake up Saturday morning,
pull on a pair of running shorts and a faded old Cubs
T-shirt, and tie my hair back in a messy French braid. I
pass Nick's closed bedroom door, behind which he'll sleep
until noon (perks of being on summer break from college),
and head downstairs for a quick breakfast of toast before I
grab my mitt and head out.

Or at least, that's the plan until I find a note stuffed

in my gym shoes. My parents know it's the only place I'll notice their messages. I bend down and pull out the wrinkled sheet of paper.

Dinner with Abram @ 6 tonight. —Mom
p.s. DRESS!!!!!

Even though she's not around to hear me, I let out a frustrated groan. For fourteen consecutive days, Mom has been reminding me that Uncle Abram's wedding is coming up and that I need to get a dress. She knows that on my list of least favorite things to do, dress shopping is in the top five. I need at least six months' notice for events requiring a dress, and Abram's invite came in with three weeks' prep.

First of all, who proposes to a woman he's been going out with for only four months? And how serious are we supposed to take it all when he hasn't even introduced his family to her yet?

Sure, that's what this dinner is for, but still…we're only meeting the fiancée and her son one week before the wedding? How dressed up do I need to be for an event that seems so poorly executed?

I toss the note in the trash and shove my feet in my shoes. On my way out the door, I text Sara that I'm on my way. By the time I get to her house—four down from mine—she's already at the foot of her driveway waiting for me, her hair tied back, her mitt on her left hand, a dog leash in the other. Our canine companion today is Moriarty, one of Sara's three Jack Russell terriers.

"Greetings, friend," Sara says as Moriarty jumps up to say hello. "You get the panic message?"

"What panic message?"

She pulls out her phone and shows me a collection of angry text messages from Joey, all including the word *sandlot* in varying degrees of uppercase letters and exclamation marks.

"He's desperate for a pitcher," Sara says.

"Clearly."

As we start toward the park, I glance across the street at Cody's house, where Mrs. Kinski's overflowing garden is bursting in an assortment of vivid reds and purples and yellows. Seeing her flowers always makes me feel happy, and I wonder if they did anything to make Cody feel better after what happened last night. I contemplate texting to ask about his diagnosis, but I suspect he'll be at the park, even though he won't be able to play with us. We're all hopeless, us four, when it comes to the sandlot. It's like a black hole, sucking us in.

It takes only about five minutes to walk to the park. This place is my proof that God exists. I pass it every day, both to and from school, and whenever I step on the brick path that winds through the park, it's like coming home. Shrieks of laughter from the playground surround me and Sara as we pass on our way to the sandlot. I swear, that playground is the Mother of All Playgrounds, sitting at the end of the path like Emerald City at the end of the Yellow Brick Road. I can recount my entire childhood through the bruises I got from horsing around there.

A couple of years ago, the park district decided to spiff up the space, making it new again to match all the modern houses going up on the other side of the subdivision. They repainted the playground blue and yellow, repaved the brick walkway, replaced the nets on the tennis courts, built a sleek pavilion with picnic tables, put a fountain at the center of the pond behind the sandlot, and built another path around the pond. The best additions were the lights they installed in the fountain, along the walkways and around the playground, so people (and by people I mean Sara, Cody, Joey, and I) could continue their park shenanigans after dark.

But the funny thing is, when they redid the park, they didn't use any of the resources to fix up the sandlot. The other funny thing is, I don't mind.

It's only a patch of sand and grass and a beat-up, old backstop, but it's my home away from home, and I wouldn't trade it for any fancy field—not even if the entire Chicago Cubs team came to my house and offered me Wrigley Field.

As Sara and I approach the sandlot, I spot Joey lying in the outfield tossing a baseball up and down. Carrot and Jiro, two other guys from the team who also live in our neighborhood, are there playing catch. Cody sits in the grass behind first base. It's not hard to miss the bright blue cast on his left forearm.

"Finally!" Joey shouts, getting to his feet. "What the hell took you so long?!" He points at Moriarty, who stares up at him. "And why the hell d'you bring this thing? You know all he does is get in the way."

Sara gestures to where Joey had been lying down. "Down, boy. Sit. Stay." She finds the bat by Cody and picks it up on her way to home plate.

"Who said you get to bat first?" Joey demands and marches over to take the bat from her. He's very possessive when it comes to baseball. And he, like me, will look for any reason to start an argument, especially with Sara. After ten years, we've all absorbed pieces one another's personalities. It's inevitable.

I go over to Cody to examine his cast up close. He looks up at me with bloodshot eyes. They complement the frown on his face.

"I must say, you look great today," I tell him.

"Shut up."

"Party at the hospital?"

"Would you like to hear the story?" he asks in a tone that makes me think I don't want to hear the story.

"I'm sure you'll tell me anyway."

"Well, first my dad decided it would be better to go to an urgent care center instead of the ER because it would be less expensive. But he couldn't remember where it was, so we drove around looking for it for half an hour, and then we had to wait, because the doctor was with another patient. And then, since I'm a wuss and wanted pain meds, we had to go to the pharmacy, where for some reason there was a *line* in the middle of the night. Then when I finally got home, frigging Reilly Shwartz next door is throwing a party, so at two o'clock in the morning, all I could hear were pounding music and shouting drunk people. Then they decide to *barbecue* in the middle of the night, and since they're all shit-housed, they burn everything, so it smells like burned hot dogs and hamburgers for the next hour. I spent all night thinking about how I'm going to exact my revenge on Santino. I might egg his house. Then fork his lawn. Then saw his arms off."

I stare at him.

This is a lot for Cody to say in one breath.

I'm about to ask why he's here if he's in such a bad mood, but something hits the small of my back. I turn to see a stick on the ground. I know without asking that Joey threw it at me.

"Pitch!" he shouts, waving his arms impatiently.

"If you need to punch something," I tell Cody, "I invite you to use Joey." I put on my mitt and head over to the mound, waving at the two sane people standing in the outfield, Carrot and Jiro. They wave back.

Carrot's real name is Garrett, but he's got fiery red hair, which is how he earned his nickname. He's a senior and works at Gilman's Sports House with my brother, Nick.

Jiro is this badass Japanese kid with spiky black hair. He's a little short, but he's one hell of a speed demon. We expect him to break the sound barrier any day now.

The six of us are the sandlot regulars. For the guys, being on the school team isn't enough. They want to play all day every day, and you can't play a pickup game with only four people. So Sara and I play with them. It took some convincing on Joey's part because, like I said, he's very possessive when it comes to baseball, and having me and Sara—the perpetual pains in his ass, like two sisters he never wanted—encroach on his space was too much for him. But once Carrot, Cody, and Jiro made him realize he couldn't make the rest of the baseball team move to our neighborhood, Joey gave in. And besides, he knows Sara and I can keep up with him. He'll just never admit it.

It's rare to find people who love what you love as much as you love it. I mean, if it was up to us, we'd spend our lives at one giant sandlot with a baseball and a bat, and we would play until the sun went out and the earth ceased to exist.

At the plate, Joey is ready—bat lifted, knees bent, eyes trained on me. He's probably trying to read my mind to see what I'm going to throw. I try confusing his telepathic skills by thinking, *Curve ball, changeup, fastball.*

I throw a fastball first. He foul-tips it over the backstop, where it lands with a *splash!* in the pond.

Over by third base, Carrot slow claps for Joey.

"Good hit," I tell Joey.

"You pitched it," he says, pulling the bat back over his shoulder.

Carrot tosses me another ball. This time I throw a slider. He fouls it over the first baseline, nearly taking out Cody's head.

"Dude, you trying to sabotage my entire baseball career?" Cody calls.

"Yeah, I thought that was Santino's job," Sara says.

Joey points the bat at me. "She pitched it."

"You know, instead of trying to blame everything on me, you could apologize," I suggest.

"What does *apologize* mean?" Joey asks.

I reposition the ball in my hand for a curve ball. "Ready to be struck out?"

"You wish."

Curve balls are my pitch. Every pitcher's got one—the pitch they throw better than the rest. Most pitchers' curves have an 11–5 trajectory, like on the hands of a clock, because it's difficult to get a perfectly vertical 12–6 drop. Thanks to Nick, I've got the 12–6 nailed. Back in his pitching days, Nick could throw his curve so it looked like it was going to be a straight shot down the middle of the plate, but at the last second, it would drop. It was his pitch, and consequently it became mine.

I like to save this pitch for special occasions, like striking Joey out. I align my feet, wind up, and throw.

Joey doesn't swing.

"Strike three!" I shout. "Suck it."

"That was a ball!"

"It was a strike!"

"Nuh-uh!"

"Uh-huh!"

"Looked like a strike from over here," Jiro says from the outfield.

"Thank you," I say. I look at Joey. "Jiro says it was a strike. So it was a strike."

"Cody!" Joey calls, seeking confirmation.

"Sorry, man, I think it was a strike."

I point at him. "I always knew I liked you."

Cody salutes me with a grin, and Joey throws the bat on the ground and sulks to the outfield.

"Someone call the waaambulance," Sara calls after him. "We've got a crybaby on the field."

"Shut up, Fox."

"Maybe I *should* ask Chizz for a spot on the team," I tease him. It comes out as a joke, but as soon as the words are out of my mouth, I realize how much I actually want to. I mean, I *did* strike out Joey.

Joey scoffs. "Like I said, gonna have to kill me first."

Despite his protests, I continue pitching, racking up strike after strike (although if you ask him for his account of the day, he'll likely say otherwise). We hardly notice that two hours pass until after Carrot runs a victory lap around the bases for hitting a home run and says, "Did anyone else hear the earthquake in my stomach?"

That draws all our attention to how hungry and thirsty we are. The sun is up high, beating down on us. Sweat drips down my neck and back. Time to call it quits.

Joey, Carrot, and Jiro, who live on the other side of the subdivision, leave together, singing "Bohemian Rhapsody" at the top of their lungs.

I tell Sara and Moriarty to go on without me, because I'm going to try and find that ball Joey hit into the pond. I'm pretty sure it landed toward the edge of the water, and

I'm not one to let a perfectly good baseball sink into a pile of mud. It takes a good five minutes of wrestling some surprisingly ferocious cattails and getting a mixture of muck and pond water in my shoes for me to retrieve it.

It also gives me a moment to dwell on who's going to take Cody's spot in the sectionals game. Since Sara jokingly nominated me for the position, I can't help but wonder what that would be like.

I was four the first time I played ball at the sandlot. Nick, who was six at the time, was starting Little League, and my dad wanted him to be the pitcher. Nick, even then, wasn't the kind of person who liked to be the center of attention. He'd rather be in the bleachers cheering for his friends. But, as it turned out, Nick was a natural.

I don't know what it was about seeing my big brother on the mound that inspired me. I do know, in those first couple of years of him owning the Little League strike zone, I wanted to be like him. He had a pitching arm gifted to him by God, but he dragged his feet to every game, threw tantrums before practices, and often bargained to clean the entire house twice a week if he could quit baseball.

Sure, he grew out of the reluctance eventually, but he never loved baseball as much as I do, which is ironic, considering he led the Corrington baseball team to the state title his senior year. Even though I love baseball in a way he never did, I lack the guts it takes to carry the responsibility of being a pitcher. Hence, the only place I ever pitch is at the sandlot, where my only real responsibility is to show up. And even then, showing up is optional.

I trudge out of the murky pond with the muddied baseball in my hand.

"Thought you might have drowned."

I'm surprised to find that Cody is waiting for me.

"Was that fun for you?" I ask, kicking some pondweed off my left shoe. "Watching me struggle? Thanks for the help by the way. I really appreciate it."

He lifts his casted arm a few inches. "Sorry. Out of order."

I frown at him. "What happened to getting that ass hat removed?"

"Doctor said he could only fix the fractured wrist. Couldn't do anything about the ass hat. Sorry."

I sigh and shake my head. "Why are you even still here?"

He holds out a clean baseball. He tosses it to me, making me drop the other ball to catch it. "I wanna show you something."

I narrow my eyes. "Show me what?"

He gives me a sly grin that makes me even more suspicious but also curious. Then he grabs my hand with his good one, which catches my heart off guard. It skips about ten beats before my brain reminds it to start pumping again.

I hardly register him pulling me to the pitcher's mound, too focused on the warmth of his calloused hand. My hand is all like, *Boy hand. Boy fingers. BOY.* And my frontal lobe is like, *Don't be stupid, hand. It's just Cody.*

Okay, so maybe when I said I'd rather be stung to death by rabid jellyfish than like him, I kind of lied. Ninety-nine percent of the time, I'm down with the jellyfish. But the other one percent of the time, when my hormones betray me like this, getting cozy with him seems so much more comfortable.

But then I remember how painfully awful it was when Joey and Sara weren't talking to each other, and how when they finally started talking to each other again, their interactions were filled with passive-aggressive gestures and angry stares.

Besides, I've held hands with Cody before. We've touched before. You can't see someone basically every day for eleven years and *not* have touched at least once.

But this is different! my hand protests.

Shut up, my brain says.

Cody drops my hand. He gestures for me to stand at the center of the mound.

I try to get a read for what he's thinking, but his face is neutral.

"Pretend you're going to pitch."

"Why?"

"Just do it, okay? I'm trying to help you."

Deciding to trust him, I position the ball in my hand, set my feet into the mound, and bring the ball to my chest. I'm about to pivot my foot when Cody grabs my right shoulder with his good hand.

"You have the worst posture I've ever seen on a pitcher."

I relax my muscles and let my hands drop to my side as I frown at him. "'Do what I say,' he said. 'I'm trying to help you,' he said," I mimic.

He laughs. "I'm getting there." He walks around to stand behind me, his hand still resting on me. My brain preemptively tells my shoulder to shut up. He pulls back, showing me how badly I was slouching. Then he moves his hand to my left shoulder and does the same.

"Big difference, right?" Before I can answer, he continues, "And when you lift your leg, keep your spine straight. You're always slouching like an old lady."

I suddenly feel really self-conscious about pitching—which hasn't happened in recent memory. Why is he doing this? To be patronizing? To make himself feel better about his fractured wrist?

"It's basic Pitching 101," he says. "That's the first thing they teach you at pitching camp."

"I went to pitching camp."

"Yeah, like, eons ago. Clearly you've forgotten

everything they taught you." He lets go of my shoulder and circles around to my front. "Okay, now pretend you're going to throw."

I don't say any of the sarcastic remarks or ask any of the very valid questions going through my mind. I just do what he says. I get into the stance, pivot my foot, bring up my knee and elbows, take my stride—

"Okay, stop," he says, grabbing my pitching arm to keep me from throwing.

Now we're in the very awkward position of me mid-pitch, with my leg outstretched, my left arm in front, my right arm in back, and him standing next to me with his hand on my bicep.

What the hell is going on?

He moves my elbow back so it's aligned with my shoulder. Then he takes my left arm in front and aligns it with home plate. "Elbow alignment. Important. It'll help your control."

This is all too much. Cody keeps his pitching secrets under a Fort Knox–level lockdown. If he starts telling me how he throws a killer changeup, I might have to tell his parents that the aliens have replaced their son with a doppelgänger.

I retract my limbs and stare at him dumbfounded.

He laughs. "Nick taught you well, but you've never had an actual coach. You've got all sorts of bad habits."

"But why did you…?"

He shrugs.

I backhand his shoulder. "Don't shrug. Why are you giving me a pitching lesson?"

"Isn't it obvious?"

"Obviously not obvious if I'm asking you why."

"I thought you'd like some pointers before you try out to be my replacement."

My heart slams to a stop. Did *Cody Kinski* just suggest I *take his place*? Hell.

I must have disbelief slapped all over my face because Cody laughs a little and says, "I know you want to."

"I was joking," I say totally unconvincingly.

He smiles. "I've known you for forever. You wouldn't give up the chance to show up a bunch of guys. And I also know that this"—he gestures to the sandlot—"isn't enough for you."

This is all true. But taking his spot on the team is daunting. He's Cody Kinski. Iron-Arm Kinski. Me pitching in his wake is laughable. Sure, I play ball recreationally way more than the average person, but no way have I logged enough competitive hours or gone to nearly enough training camps to play on Chizz's team. No matter how the scene might play out in my imagination, in reality, I'd walk onto the field at tryouts, and every last person alive will die of laughter.

Would it be nice to be standing on the mound, smack in the center of the infield, taking down the patriarchy with my killer arm, crowd cheering as I pitch us to victory? Yeah, probably.

But then there's the *other* possibility: choking. Completely screwing up. That's too much pressure.

I mean, I know I'm good. But I'm not *Iron-Arm Kinski* good. Not good enough to carry the weight of expectation that comes with playing at sectionals. Maybe for a regular season game that doesn't have much consequence (and let me emphasize *maybe*), but this is asking too much.

The hypothetical idea of playing on Chizz's team might be alluring, but in reality, I couldn't do it. The proof of that reality is in the scoreboard of the last softball game I ever played. I will never get the image of that scoreboard out of my mind.

"That is all…very…ridiculous," I tell Cody unconvincingly.

The corners of his lips turn up. He starts off the field. "Not *that* ridiculous."

I stand on the mound for a moment, taking all this in, before following him.

I don't want to believe him.

But even more than that, I do.

4

RIGHT BEFORE WE'RE ABOUT TO LEAVE FOR dinner with Abram, an email pops into my school inbox. It's a mass email to the entire school from the Corrington High School Athletic Department. Subject: *Varsity pitching tryouts Monday 3:45*.

It's obviously meant for guys who are already on the varsity team or who are on the fresh-soph or JV teams.

Not for outsiders and not for girls.

"Marnie!" Mom calls from downstairs. "You ready to go? We're leaving in five!"

I look down at the sweatpants and tank top I put on after my shower. I shut my laptop and get up to rummage through my closet. I don't suppose throwing on a T-shirt will suffice. Not for Mom, who's big on good first impressions and who has been desperately trying to get some nicer clothes in my closet for the last five years.

I find a pair of black skinny jeans and a red tunic top I borrowed from Sara and never gave back. Downstairs, Mom is in a panic, trying to find her keys, get Nick to put on a tie, and fix her bun. Hoping to avoid any criticism of my haphazard fashion choices, I slip past her as she sics Dad on Nick, and I head to the car in the garage.

Later, on the way to the restaurant, I confer with the familial unit about my dilemma.

"On the one hand," I say, after telling them the situation, "I could play for real on a real team in a real game—I mean, *if* I can even get on the team and *if* girls are even allowed to play on a boys' team. But on the other hand, I don't do well in real games."

Silence fills the car as the three of them mull this over. I know we're thinking about a very specific day—May 30, almost exactly twenty-four months ago, my freshman year of high school. Sara and I were the only two freshmen to make the varsity softball team, her for her mad sprint times, me for my arm. We'd made it to regionals, mostly due to Brynn Loren, who had a .810 batting average (the second highest nationally) and was known as not only our cleanup batter, but as our janitorial queen. She cleared the bases like it was nobody's business. If she was on the opposing team and I had to pitch against her, I'd probably run the other way.

In the seventh inning of that game, after I let two batters get on base and the third hit a three-run homer, I really did run the other way. Away from softball. Away from competitive sports. Away from team sports. Away from my teammates. Even though they all patted me on the back, saying, "It's cool, Marnie. It wasn't your fault," I knew it was. Home runs always felt like my fault.

In Little League, I got upset when we lost, but those feelings would go away after a bowl of ice cream and some video games. After that regionals game, I was below rock bottom for nearly two months. I don't know why I let it get to me so much. Maybe it was because I hate losing or because I hated that thirteen other girls lost because of me or because it was a reminder that I wasn't good enough or maybe it was all of the above.

"No harm in trying out," Dad says. Of course that's what Dad would say. Dad would do anything to have a kid on the team again. He would never admit it, but I know he misses coming to our games, setting up the lawn chairs off the sidelines, drinking an iced coffee, and chatting up other players' parents.

"Chizz probably wants someone on the team," Nick says. "Or someone from JV."

"But he sent an email to the entire school," I remind him.

"Probably 'cause he couldn't figure out how to send it to only the guys on the teams. As I recall, Chizz and technology are like oil and water. Anyway, the tryouts are likely for backup in case the relief pitchers fall through."

"We've only got one relief pitcher." It was a gamble on Chizz's part, having only one backup. He didn't want anyone but Cody on the mound. But if need be, Ray Torres would step up. Except, he's pitched only two games the entire season. Jiro is *technically* a relief pitcher too, but he's never pitched a game this season.

"To be honest," Nick says, "I think the *guys* who are on the baseball teams—varsity or JV—will get priority over, well...*you*."

"Spoken like a male baseball player," Dad teases. "Marnie, you should try out. To hell with the boys. We all know what an arm you've got. And hey, I'm sure Chizz would love to have a Locke on the team again."

"A *Nick* Locke," I say. "Not a *Marnie* Locke."

Back in his day, Nick was the Cody Kinski of the Corrington baseball team—the pitcher with a reputation to make the opposing team quiver in their cleats. Chizz loved Nick so much, I honestly thought he might propose. When I got to high school, Chizz probably thought I'd be as badass as Nick, but he found out I'm mostly just a *pain* in the ass.

Dad looks over his shoulder from the front seat. "Like I said, no harm."

"Except being laughed in the face by a bunch of egotistical jocks," I say.

"Hey, you've grown up with Nick, Joey, *and* Cody," Dad reminds me. "Surely you've developed a thick enough layer of skin."

Trying out for the baseball team would be the real test of that.

I'm about to ask Nick how *he* would've reacted if a girl tried out for his team, but a song I don't know comes on the radio, and Nick says, "Oh, hey, I love this song. Turn it up."

The conversation ends.

All the while, Mom stays silent in the driver's seat, her eyes fixed on the road ahead, focusing on anything but me talking about trying out for the baseball team. Let's just say Mom got the short end of the stick when it comes to having common interests with her daughter. Based on the photographs from her college days and the conversations I've overheard with her girlfriends, she would've rather had a daughter who liked to go shopping, have makeover nights, and watch rom coms with her. Sometimes I think she feels cheated. Dad got two kids who inherited his athleticism, his love for baseball, his sense of humor, his tallness, and his big brown eyes. All Nick inherited from

Mom was her neat-freak tendencies, and all I got was her reddish-brown hair. I didn't even get the waves. Dad taught me how to bat and throw, and, well, Mom never even got a chance to teach me how to use a straightener.

To be honest, I'd rather have the bat.

The restaurant is one of those dimly lit, sit-down places with waiters clad in black and white, mini chandeliers hanging over each table, and special dessert menus that are as long as the ones for the main courses. I partly suspect Abram chose the place so he could feed us ginormous servings of lasagna, tortellini, ravioli, and the best tiramisu known to mankind so we wouldn't inspect his fiancée too closely.

Inside, Mom leads us through the crowded waiting area to the hostess stand and tells the host that we have a reservation under Barclay. He gestures for us to follow him.

As we weave through tables piled high with drool-inducing Italian food, Mom quietly reminds us all (mainly me) to behave, and by that, she means I should think before I speak so I don't surprise anyone with how sharp my tongue can be. I'm hardly listening. All I can think about is how happy my stomach is going to be.

The host leads us to a table all the way in the back. My

attention shifts to Abram's fiancée and her son. I'm not sure what to expect. Mom said Geanna is a fashion designer. As for her son, I know zip about him, not even how old he is. Nick has three inches on me, so I don't get a visual until we are almost table side. I stop dead in my tracks.

Dad runs into me.

"Hey," he says, "remember when we taught you how to walk about sixteen years ago?"

I ignore him and swallow the *What the hell?* on my tongue because sitting between my uncle and my soon-to-be aunt is Santino Acardi.

———

Santino frigging Acardi. Psychotic, malicious, demon pitcher! Here! My...*cousin-to-be.* I must have done something *really* awful to have been dealt this hand.

I don't know how long I stand there, Santino and me staring at each other. Is he staring because he recognizes me for nearly starting a fight with his baseball team or because I'm going to be his cousin? He's smiling at least. But is it fake?

Either way, he's the bastard who fractured Cody's wrist and benched him for the postseason. And even before this last game, Santino has been the bane of Cody's high school baseball career. From the brushbacks to the unnecessary condescension to the giant ego, Santino has relentlessly and successfully played the part of archnemesis.

Mom clears her throat and gestures at the chair between her and Nick. Translation: *Sit down before they think you're weird.*

I slide into the seat and turn my attention to Geanna. She definitely wears the look of a fashion designer with her perfectly curled hair, manicured nails, and tight, silky, expensive-looking electric blue top. She's smiling pearly white teeth and looks nice enough, but what does any of that matter when her spawn is frigging *Santino Acardi*?

Under the table, someone kicks my shin.

I bite back my yelp and glare at the culprit.

Mom.

She throws me another look. *Say something!*

Right. Because I'm supposed to act friendly.

But he wrecked Cody's wrist! My brain protests. *To hell with civility! Deck the bastard!*

Interestingly enough, I never knew how loyal I was to Cody until just now.

Mom clears her throat again.

"Hi," I say. So lame.

At least it initiates the introductions. Abram goes around saying names, then a lot of useless small talk takes place, and while everyone else seems to get along easily, I stew in my newfound dilemma.

I'm loyal to Cody, yes, but I'm also loyal to my mom, my bearer of flesh and blood, who wants more than anything right now for us all to be one big happy family. Mom and Abram are the closest out of their four siblings. Abram used to come around all the time when he worked at an industrial design studio, which was close to us. But after he started traveling for work, he cut his semimonthly visits to only Christmas. Apparently that's his excuse for not having us all meet earlier. Both he and Geanna have been too busy earning frequent flyer miles from their jobs.

When I tune back in, Geanna is saying, "Santino's girlfriend would have come too, but she had to teach a guitar lesson tonight."

Girlfriend?

The fiend has a significant other? What kind of demon must *she* be?

"Neha's practically part of our family," Geanna continues. "I think you guys will really love her."

"She's a riot," Abram adds with a laugh. "In a good way."

I don't know what to make of this. Santino has a girlfriend, and my uncle, who I greatly admire, approves of her. I believe in some twisted way that means Santino, in a surprising turn of events, might actually not be a crony of the devil…?

"So, Marnie," Abram says. "I was telling Santino that you and Nick have a lot in common with him."

Other than the fact that we are all *Homo sapiens*?

I'd rather have more in common with a crocodile.

I study Abram's fingers tapping on the edge of the table. Usually he's so chill, but I can practically *smell* the nervousness on him. He, like Mom, wants this to be a success. Little does he know it's already an epic fail.

"He said you guys are big fans of baseball," Santino chimes in. He looks at me and Nick as if he's not sure who to look it. Is he nervous, too? Is Santino Acardi, notoriously cocky asshole, nervous? I wouldn't be surprised if he's putting on a show for Abram and Geanna before he murders us all with an ax.

Mom nudges my shin again.

"Yes. I like baseball," I say. I sound like *I'm* about to murder someone with an ax.

"Cubs or Sox?" Santino asks.

It's such an innocent question that I can't tell if he's pretending not to recognize me from Friday night or if he really doesn't remember. Does Geanna know her son benched another guy for the most important part of his baseball career thus far? I mean, considering Santino's affront to Cody wasn't deemed "malicious" by the ump, she *could* think it was an accident. It's baseball. People get hit sometimes.

"Cubs," I say flatly. Mom shoots me another look. *Why do you have to sound so cold?*

I'm saved from more icy conversation by the waiter, who comes to ask us what we'd like to drink (waters all round) and if we'd like any appetizers (eggplant bruschetta and fried mushrooms). When he leaves, Abram turns the conversation to Geanna's new store opening up at the Corrington Terrace soon. That leads to questions about whether Dad is going to open up a second restaurant, which leads to questions about how Dad's current restaurant is doing. We would have gone there tonight, but Abram and Geanna are saving Dad's master chef skills for the wedding. As we wait for our appetizers, Dad tells the story about how he had to fire one of his chefs for being stoned on the job.

Multiple times throughout dinner, between bites of my four-cheese ravioli and minestrone soup, I have the strongest urge to jump out of my seat and shout at Santino, "Why did you do it?! Why are you such an arrogant piece of shit?! Why couldn't you just let Cody be?!"

But I bite it back, which, for me, is like trying not to scratch an itch.

"So," Abram says toward the end of dinner when all our stomachs are stuffed. "Geanna and I have some big news."

I can't help it. "Is it that you're getting married?" I say dryly.

"No, smarty-pants." Abram turns to Geanna. "Would you like to tell them?"

She leans forward. "Well…I…" She smiles wide, draws in a breath, and then gushes, "I'm pregnant!"

"Really?" we all say, but Mom's voice is the loudest. Her eyes are wide. It's like she can't understand how her little brother could possibly *impregnate* a woman.

Abram smiles sheepishly. "Yes, really."

No wonder they're getting married so quickly. It's a shotgun wedding.

"We've started putting the nursery together," Geanna says. For some reason, it shocks me that they are already living together. It makes this union tangible. Inevitable. Geanna's bubbliness triples, as if this—the baby—is what she's waited to talk about all evening. "It's going to—"

"Anyone want the rest of my tiramisu?" Santino interrupts. He lifts the plate with the half-eaten cake and offers it to each of us. It's like if he doesn't get rid of it *now* he'll die. Strange. But not as strange as him offering it to me the longest.

I shake my head, afraid that if I speak, I'll wind up saying something mean. I'm not sure there's a passive-aggressive way to decline tiramisu, but I'm sure my mouth would find a way before my brain stops it.

"Marnie, you love tiramisu," Mom says. Her eyes scream, *Take the peace offering! Take it now!*

"No thanks," I say.

Mom shifts in her seat. She knows something is wrong—I never say no to tiramisu.

Santino retracts the plate, defeated, like he's been rejected from the family too. My cold introduction, lack of chitchat over dinner, and now this refusal must make him aware that I hate him. I mean, if Cody, who is typically the chillest of us all, was ready to egg his house, fork his lawn, *and* saw the dude's arms off, then I see no reason not to dislike him.

Well, besides the fact that he's going to be my cousin…

I can't even look at his face without wanting to punch him. He might look harmless now, but that doesn't erase the countless times I've seen his conniving smirk, and it will be a very, *very* long time before I forget the look on Cody's face when he got hit by Santino's pitch. Cody's not even the only one who felt the force of that pitch. Chizz felt it too, and the whole team and his parents and Sara.

And me.

"I have to go to the bathroom," I say way more abruptly than I mean to. I can feel Mom's frustration as I push my chair back and stand.

In the restroom, there's a line for the three toilet stalls. Not that it matters. I'm not here to relieve myself. I pull out my phone and start texting Sara.

But how do I word this? How do I ease her into the news? What would Sara say, anyway? She'd probably encourage me to run a fork through Santino's chest.

"Um, are you going to use the bathroom or not?" an old lady snaps at me.

"Sorry," I mumble, stepping back outside the bathroom without sending the text.

I run straight into Santino.

"Whoa, what the hell?" I snap at him. "Are you *following me*?"

"Sorry. Didn't mean to scare you," he says.

I narrow my eyes at him but don't say anything. Now is not the time to start a scene. I try to sidestep him, but Santino says, "So what's the deal?"

I gape at him. "What deal?"

He shrugs, almost sheepishly. "I don't know, I just…get the feeling you don't like me."

The insecurity in his voice doesn't match the arrogance I associate with him. "What do you care if I like you or not?"

I try to step around him again, but he goes, "Because we're going to be cousins." Like I haven't figured that out. "Look, I don't know what your problem is, but I really want this to work out. For my mom. And you should too, for your uncle."

So he doesn't remember me from yesterday.

I can't play nice any longer. "My problem is you're an asshole."

Suddenly his face turns cold. It's the look he has every time he steps onto the mound at a game. "Well, maybe from my point of view, *you're* being the asshole."

He still doesn't get it. I cross my arms. "Fine. You wanna know what my problem is? First, you let your teammate get away with being a complete asswipe to not only me, but my best friend. And second, you purposely hit Cody with that pitch, and now he can't play for the rest of postseason. That's exactly the kind of asshole move that makes me resent that we're going to be family."

Realization dawns on his face as he takes this all in. "You're friends with Cody."

"You fractured his wrist," I say, "and you better be glad I don't tell your mom or Abram what a dick you are."

"You don't even know me."

"I know you think you're some baseball god who can throw brushbacks at people for the hell of it, and that two years ago when Cody was chosen over you to be pitcher for the all-star team, you went online and tried to convince people that Cody had bribed the coaches."

He looks taken aback that I know this but doesn't hesitate to defend himself. "I was a dumb freshman when I made those posts, okay? I was jealous. It happens."

"*Was* jealous? You mean you *are* jealous, and you think you can sabotage Cody for being better than you." A woman coming out of the bathroom stares at us as she walks past, most likely because my voice is becoming steadily louder. I lower it as I glare at him. "Look, I don't like you, and I don't want to be your cousin. But for the sake of my mom and my uncle, I'll put up with you. Just don't try to be my friend, or we're going to have some real problems."

Before a real argument breaks out, I push past him and head back to our table. A few moments later, he returns, too. He doesn't make any eye contact with me. Maybe it's because he knows that one wrong look and I'll tell his mom and future stepfather what he did to Cody.

Thanks to Cody, we both transitively despise each other, but my prejudice won't scare him. Of course it won't—he *is* Santino Acardi. He's not going to be afraid of a hundred-and-ten-pound loudmouthed girl.

The question is: should *I* be afraid of *him*?

5

BEFORE SCHOOL ON MONDAY, I GO TO THE atrium in the library. That's where we hang out before homeroom. I kept the events of Saturday's dinner to myself all weekend, trying to figure out how to break it to everyone gently. As I head to our table under the skylight, I have every intention of telling Sara about it, but when I get there, I find she's not alone.

"Hello, Marnie," Joey says in a suspiciously formal tone.

I slide my backpack onto the table. "Hello, Joseph."

"So," he says, "you're going right home after school today, yes?"

Sara shakes her head as she weaves strings for a rope toy she's making for her dogs. "He's been complaining for the past fifteen minutes about how he doesn't want you to try out."

I take a seat next to Sara. "Who said I was trying out?"

In answer, Joey gestures over my shoulder. I turn. Cody's in the print lab on the other side of the library.

In addition to stressing over the whole Santino issue yesterday, I also spent an unhealthy amount of time on Google learning about girls who have played on boys' baseball teams. I went back and forth on if I should try out. The last thing I did was watch that unspeakable YouTube video someone posted of the last play of my last softball game. The one of me completely botching up, just to remind myself of the pain of ultimate failure. I had to close the window before the ending.

"You're going straight home after school," Joey insists.

Even though I know that I will indeed be going home straight after school, I tease him just because it's fun. "What?" I say with a smirk, "you worried I'm going to start a one-woman crusade against your team and overthrow your reign as captain?"

"I'm dead serious. Don't do it."

"Why not?" Of course, I know why I shouldn't—stress, failure, embarrassment, etc. But I would like to hear it from a member of the team.

"What do you mean, 'Why not?'" he asks. "You've been butting into everything I do my entire life. Can't you find your own thing for once?"

I raise my eyebrows in confusion. "What the hell are you talking about?"

"Let's take a gander, shall we? In third grade, I wanted to research marine animals for my science project, but then you stole the topic from me. In fifth grade, I wanted to be Paul Revere in the school play, and you stole that from me too. In seventh grade, I said I wanted to learn how to play piano, and then suddenly *you* wanted to play the piano too. And then last year, when Cody and I wanted to do that April Fools' Day joke on Sara with the water balloons, you invited yourself along and then took credit for it. Now this. Why do you have to go and insert yourself in my thing *again?*"

"All 'That's what she said' jokes aside, that is ridiculous." But even as I say it, I realize I do stuff like that to him all the time.

Sara clears her throat. "And there *was* the time you were going out with Ling Wu, who broke up with you because she turned out to be gay, which she realized only after admitting she was more attracted to Marnie that she was to you…"

Joey glares at us as we stifle laughs. "Yes," he says, gritting his teeth, "and there's *that.*"

"Don't forget Ling is now dating Brie," Cody says, dropping himself in the seat between me and Joey. "Brie, your *other* ex-girlfriend."

At that, I completely bust up.

Joey shoots us all the middle finger.

"So," Cody says, "are we reliving Joey's entire sucky streak of relationships? Did we talk about…" He leans forward and looks directly at Sara.

"Fuck off," she tells him.

Cody sits back in his chair. "It was worth a shot."

"What we *were* talking about," Joey says, "was *her*. And how she's going to try and *invade* our team." He backhands Cody's shoulder. "No thanks to your encouragement." He stands up abruptly.

"Where are you going?" Cody asks.

"Gotta go print something," Joey says, pulling Cody's shirt.

"But—" Cody doesn't get to finish before Joey yanks him off back to the print lab.

"What the hell's his deal?" I ask when they're out of earshot.

"He's Joey," Sara says, as if that explains his behavior. Which, I suppose, in a way, it does. Joey is possessive about baseball. It's what he lives for. It's *his thing*. And obviously he doesn't want me stepping all over him. But to hold grudges against me for stuff I did back in third grade? That's harsh.

"So are you going to try out?" Sara asks. "I really think you should. No joking."

I know she means it. I mean, Sara's always supportive, but she knows how much anxiety I got playing softball.

After we lost that fateful game, she spent the majority of her time dragging me off the sofa to cheer me up. So when she says I should try out, she's not saying it just to say it.

"Do you really think I could do it?" I ask. "Do you think the *guys* would let me do it?"

"To your first question: yes. We played on the same softball team, and I see you pitch at the sandlot. And to your second question: who cares? What do you have to lose, anyway?"

"My dignity, for one."

She laughs. "Well, if *my* opinion doesn't count, take Cody's. You know he wants the team to go to state more than anyone. And if he endorses you as his replacement…" Sara goes back to tying her dog toy. "Man, I would love to see Santino's face if he saw that his attempt to thwart our team from state was itself thwarted…by a *girl*."

Santino.

Right. Because there's *that* problem too.

"What's wrong?" Sara asks immediately.

I take a deep breath and lean across the table, gesturing for her to get closer.

"What?" she repeats.

"I've got something to tell you," I whisper.

"Ooo, gossip time," she says excitedly as she puts the dog toy aside. "My favorite part of the day."

And then, as quietly as I can, lest anyone be listening in, I tell her about the dinner with Abram, Geanna, and Santino.

Her jaw drops. "And let me guess, you haven't told Cody."

I shake my head.

"You have to! Right now!" She points at the computer lab, where Joey and Cody stand over a printer.

"And be branded a traitor for the rest of my life? No thanks."

"He needs to hear it from you," she says. "You've got to rip off the Band-Aid. I mean, why *not* tell him?"

"Cody's already upset about his arm and not being able to play, and I don't want to pile it on. I mean, Santino and I are going to be *related*. Cousins. Or cousins once removed. Or step-cousins. Hell, I don't know. But the fetus growing in Geanna's uterus will be my cousin. Related by blood. This is a lifelong deal, and we all have to get along. What if Cody takes out his anger at Santino on me?"

"Cody wouldn't do that. You need to tell him."

I bite my lip. "I don't know what Santino is like off the field yet, either. What if he starts taking out *his* jealousy and hatred for Cody on me?"

"That's Santino's problem. Not Cody's. You need to tell him. And I wouldn't wait too long."

I give a tentative nod. "I know."

I look over at the print lab, where Cody and Joey are in conversation. Based on their concentration, it seems like they're arguing. Then Cody looks up, straight at me. A small grin appears on the corner of his lips, like he's pleased to have caught me watching him.

If he's smiling, maybe he's not in a bad mood, and I can tell him about Santino. But as soon as he turns back to Joey, his grin fades, and he's got irritation written all over his face.

I sigh.

Sara nudges my arm. "You know, from over here, the contours of Cody's muscles look pretty badass. I mean, look at those calves. Damn."

I snap my head toward her. *"What?"*

"Or was it his sexily disheveled hair you were ogling?"

"I wasn't ogling."

She scoffs. "Okay."

"I wasn't!"

"If you say so."

"*You* were the one who brought up the sexy hair and muscles."

"But I was reading your mind."

"Stop." Like I've got time to worry about her playing cupid between tryouts and Santino.

She cackles. Yes, cackles. As only Sara can. "You're *blushing*, Marnie."

"Shut up. I don't care what you think you know about me or him. There's *nothing* there."

"I beg to differ. You're all flustered. There's *something* there, but you are chicken. And *he's* chicken. And two chickens don't make an un-chicken."

"Shut up."

She does, but she's still got a satisfied smirk on her face.

And damn, does my face feel hot.

6

CODY'S PRETTY ATTRACTIVE, I GUESS. I MEAN, IT'S not something you really notice when you grow up with someone. It's like, every day you see them and nothing changes, but then one day, you just look at them and you're like, *wow*, and you want to go to their parents' house and congratulate them on their successful mix of DNA.

He's got nice eyes. They're not sparkly blue or bright green. They're just brown. Light brown. So light that sometimes they look almost orange in the sun. Not that I spend an enormous amount of time staring into his eyes. I just noticed once or twice. And maybe a few more times after that.

He's kind of buff too. Not like a weight-lifting burly type of buff, but he's got nice, lean muscles that you can't help but want to run your hands over. Not that I've ever done that, but you know, I'm only human. Sometimes I think things.

"What are you staring at?"

I tear my gaze away from Cody's left calf.

"Nothing."

We got a free period in English today after we turned in our papers. AP testing finished last week, so all our classes are pretty much do-whatever-the-hell-you-want. Cody and I asked Mrs. Sorren if we could go to the library. She didn't care, and here we are.

We're sitting in the same place as this morning. I thought I'd wanted to get away from our rowdy class, but apparently I just wanted to stare at Cody's legs.

He raises an eyebrow at me, and I think he can see into my mind. I'm afraid he's going to accuse me of checking him out, but all he says is, "So you ready to show off your mad pitching skills to Chizz?"

I wanted a change of subject but not *this* subject. "That's a loaded question," I say.

"You have to at least try out."

"Why would I subject myself to that kind of pressure when I would turn him down in the end?"

"*That's* a loaded question."

"No, it's not."

"Turning down Chizz suggests you expect him to offer you the position." Cody rests his elbows on the table and leans forward. "What are you so freaked out about, anyway? You're always bragging about how good you are."

"Only because it's fun to brag. I don't actually *mean* it." Talking the talk is indeed easier than walking the walk.

He throws me a *bullshit* look.

"Okay, so maybe I'm a good pitcher. But I'm not you."

"You don't have to be."

"Everyone on the team will want me to be." I remember what Joey said this morning. "Not even Joey will be on my side."

Cody doesn't refute this. "He's just worried you'll choke again, but—"

"*What?* I thought he didn't want me to intrude."

Cody cringes, like he realizes he shouldn't have said anything about Joey.

I backhand his shoulder. "Joey thinks I'm gonna choke?"

He shrugs. "Well…his exact words were, 'We'll lose if she pitches.'"

I nearly shoot out of my chair. "*What?*"

"Marnie—"

"That unsupportive asshole. And here I thought he was just being possessive."

"He's that too."

"After all the ball we've played together, he doesn't think I could do it. If he's worried about me getting on the team, doesn't that negate the fact that he thinks I suck?"

"He doesn't think you suck. He thinks you'd make the team, but he doesn't think you can handle the pressure since you haven't played on a team in so long, and since you haven't played on *our* team."

I sit back in my chair, mulling this over. They are valid concerns. But still. After I've gone to all his games, played ball with him at the park, let him copy off my homework…

One time I mess up, and he thinks I'll always choke.

I stand, picking up my backpack.

"Where are you going?" Cody asks.

"To pay Joey a visit."

"There are still ten minutes before the bell."

"I'll wait for him outside his classroom."

Cody sighs. "You don't have to go running to pick a fight every time someone insults you."

"Oh, it's not *someone*. It's Joey."

"Don't you think you've fought with him enough over the years to let this go?"

"That's exactly the reason I shouldn't." I've learned a

lot about my friends over the years, and this is what I've learned about Joey: you have to give him a piece of your mind, or he'll keep walking all over you. And I am not one to be walked over.

"Marnie—"

"Stay here if you don't want to pick sides. I'll see you at lunch."

"Marnie—"

But I ignore him and head out of the library. I'm not going to try out for the dumb baseball team, but I'm going to let Joey know that it's not because he doesn't want me to.

———

When the bell rings signaling the end of fourth period, Joey is the first one out of his Spanish classroom. He's talking to Brie—who he is still majorly lovestruck by and close with even though they broke up. I grab the sleeve of his shirt and pull him to the side of the hallway by the windows.

"So you think I'd choke," I say, not even trying to hide the accusation in my voice.

He lets out an annoyed huff. I don't know if it's because of what I said or because Brie has continued down the hall, not even giving him a second glance. Then he says, "I knew Cody would tell you."

"And you think I'd make the team lose."

"Probably just to spite me too."

"You know, a few days ago, you were desperate for me to pitch for you at the sandlot."

Just then, Sara emerges from a classroom down the hall. She spots me and Joey, and scurries over. "What's going on?" she asks, sounding nervous because she knows shit is about to go down.

"That was different," Joey says, ignoring her. "That was for *fun*. *This* is for *real*."

I cross my arms. "You don't think I could pitch for fun *and* for real?"

"Guys…" Sara says, then nods at the staring bystanders.

Joey stands up straighter. "No, I don't. Because I know you, Marnie. You like to play the big shot, but you get scared as easily as anyone else. You can't live up to the better-than-thou shit that comes out of your mouth. Remember that softball game? Like I'd let that happen at our sectionals game and ruin our chances to get to state."

All the muscles in my body tense as the rage surges through me. This is so classic Joey, insulting me because he can't think of a better way to process his emotion, like, oh, I don't know, *being a rational person.*

"You know I'm right," he says. "That's why you've got nothing to say." Then he walks away.

I start weaving through the crowd of students after him, and Sara pulls on my backpack. "Marnie, don't listen to—"

I yank away from her and catch up to Joey, matching his long strides.

"You're not helping your case," I snap at him. "You should know better than anyone that telling me I *can't* do something is the best way to make me do it. I *was* going to tell you that I wasn't going to try out and that it wasn't because you didn't want me to. Except now I think I will. And when Chizz chooses me, and we win sectionals, then you'll have no choice but to admit that you were wrong."

He stops abruptly and snaps at me, "You've got a big mouth on a big head, and I definitely know I'm not wrong about that. But *fine*, play if you think you can. Just don't expect any special treatment just because Cody personally requested you take his spot. We all know his crush on you makes him biased."

Normally I'd freak out over that five-letter C-word, especially coming from the mouth of Cody's best friend, but I know it's not true. Joey will say anything to provoke me. I won't rise to it. "You know what I think?"

"Not really, and I don't particularly care," he retorts.

"I think you can't stand me doing anything better than you."

"I can't stand you being a bigheaded prat."

"Takes one to know one, *Joseph*."

"Guys!" Sara shouts, shoving us apart. "You are in public! Act civilized, for God's sake!"

"*Jerk*," I snarl at Joey.

"*Takes one to know one*," he mocks.

I make a lunge to shove him, but Sara pulls me back again. "Marnie!"

Around us, some kids start chanting, "Fight, fight, fight, fight—"

"Keep walking, freshies!" Sara shouts at them, pulling me away from Joey, who stalks off. "What is with you?" she asks, basically dragging me down the hall. "It's just Joey."

I stay silent and let her pull me along to the caf. Joey also has lunch this period, and even though we always sit together, I have a feeling he's not going to be making an appearance today.

In a way, I should probably thank him. I've made my decision. Maybe I *am* a bigheaded prat with a loud mouth and no substance. Or maybe the real reason I don't want to try out is because I'm afraid I'll choke.

So after school, I make a beeline to the girls' locker room, put on my gym clothes, and psyche myself up for tryouts. Maybe to show Joey that I can make the team. Or maybe just to show myself.

7

ON THE FIRST DAY OF KINDERGARTEN, I WAS one extremely pissed off five-year-old.

Here's why.

Nick was going into first grade, and he wanted the electric-blue backpack that my mom bought on clearance at Target. But *I* wanted the electric-blue backpack too. So we're screaming at each other, playing tug-of-war with it, while my mom shouts at us to stop, because there is only one blue backpack. But after she wrangles it away from us, she gives it to Nick because he's older, and I get the stupid red backpack that he used the year before.

Then on the ride to kindergarten, my mom says she's not going to stay with me at this new place. There's going to be other kids my age and a teacher who's going to take care of us, and I'm supposed to listen to this teacher and do what she says. But my mom's not going to be there with me. She's *leaving me.*

We pull into the parking lot at the school, and I can already tell it's gonna suck. There's a dingy, little playground on the side—nothing compared to the playground by my house. They're going to make me play on that pathetic playground. I just know it.

My mom drags me out of the car, and the only reason I'm not crying is because I spent all my tears on the blue backpack that I didn't get.

Inside, we find my classroom, where fifteen other kids are already running around, throwing blocks at one another, eating crayons, and crying for Mommy.

A tall woman with red hair and glasses comes over and talks to my mom, and then she kneels down so she's at my eye level. "Hi, Marnie. My name is Mrs. Walburn. I think we're going to be really good friends this year."

Even five-year-old me knows she's lying through her teeth, so I grab my mom's leg and tell her to take me home.

After much prying and pleading, my mom removes me from her leg, sits me down at a table, and tells me to be good. No fighting, she says. Then she says it again: "*No fighting.*"

And then she's gone.

Mrs. Walburn suggests I go play blocks with the nice little boy with the blond hair who is stacking blocks like he's going to be the next Frank Lloyd Wright.

So, silly me, I do what she says. Without talking to him, I sit and start making my own tower.

He glances at my tower, and I glance at his, and the next thing I know, we've silently established a competition for the tallest building. His is almost his height. Mine's getting there too. He eyes my tower enviously. He eyes me suspiciously. And you know what the little runt does?

He *backs into my tower, collapsing it like the Holy Roman Empire.* Totally on purpose too.

That was the last straw. I didn't get my backpack. My mom left me. And this jerk face knocked over my tower. I shove him, hard, and he stumbles into his own masterpiece. He and it fall in one swift *timberrr!*

And that, my friends, is the story of how I met Joseph Myrtall.

———

"I want to hang him by his toes and beat the pulp out of him," I say as I dig through the bag of school mitts in the equipment room.

"Well, you're always saying he's the second brother you never had," Cody says, drawing on his cast with a Sharpie.

"And here I thought my fights with Nick were bad."

"He'll come around. You know he always does."

I throw aside another mitt that's too big. "I should've run home to get my own."

Cody kneels beside me and pulls one out. He gives it to me.

I try to take it from him, but he doesn't let go. "What?"

His gaze lingers on me for a second longer than necessary before he releases the mitt. "Nothing."

"If you think this is a bad idea, let me know now please."

He shakes his head.

I slip my left hand into the mitt. It fits perfectly. "Then what?"

He bites his lip, drawing my attention to how soft his lips look.

Dammit. Not now.

"I'm just glad you're doing this" is all he says.

I give my mitt a few punches to get a feel for it. "I don't even know if I'm allowed to try out," I say.

"I'm sure Chizz will find a loophole once he sees how badass you are." He smiles, but it doesn't reach his eyes.

I put the rejected mitts back in the bag. "Okay, what is with you?"

"What?"

We leave the equipment room. "I mean this whole thing with you pretending it doesn't bother you that you got injured, then trying to be happy, but then also fighting with Joey when you think Sara and I aren't looking and"—I gesture at his cast—"scrawling emo spirals of doom in black Sharpie."

"I don't know what you're talking about," he says, and pushes open the door to the fields, inviting fresh air into the hallway. When I don't follow him out, he steps back inside.

"Cody Alexander Kinski, how long have I known you?"

He grins a little at the sound of me whipping out his full name.

"Right. Eleven years," I answer for him. "There is nothing you can hide from me."

"I think you should focus on tryouts. And you should get there early so that Chizz has time to process you being there."

"For example," I continue, ignoring him. "I know that you hate apple juice. That you always tie your left shoe first. And you still have that Build-A-Bear with the Cubs jersey that Sara and I gave you for your fourteenth birthday, and he has his own little bed, which you and Joey made him out of a shoe box, in your closet. I also know that you're afraid of being buried alive, and that you always sleep with an arm under your pillow, so you probably haven't been sleeping very well these past few days. And I know that sometimes—and by sometimes, I mean all the time—you don't want people to feel bad for you or to worry about you or even notice when you're having a hard time. But I know when something is wrong, because, to be honest, you're not very good at hiding it."

He doesn't seem surprised that I know all this. Surely he knows as much about me, if not more.

"If you know me so well, then you should know what's wrong." He pushes the door open again and gestures for me to go outside. "But like I said, I think you've got other stuff to worry about right now."

Just then, a door connected to the boys' locker room bursts open and a bunch of guys from the team spill outside, all rowdy and excited. They don't notice me and Cody, but it's impossible not to notice them. The sight of them—all the muscles and tans and jockness—makes my stomach turn. Suddenly, comforting Cody falls right off my list of priorities. Going home starts sounding like a great idea.

A rough but gentle hand slips itself into mine. "Don't be intimidated by them. Our team is a bunch of softies." He drops his hand and adds, "For the most part."

I would definitely not categorize *Joey* as a softie. Even Carrot and Jiro are a stretch.

"Why do you want me to do this so badly?" I ask him.

"Because I want our team to win."

I raise an eyebrow.

"Okay, *and* because it would be a real nice 'F you' to Santino. He probably thinks he can take down our team by taking me down, but for us to come back with *you* in my place? I mean, no offense, but you're not the most intimidating person, as much as you like to think you are."

At the mention of Santino, my heart lurches in my chest. I've still gotta tell him about *that*.

"Why does it matter what Santino thinks anyway?" I ask, hoping to ease Cody into my confession. "He's already out of the play-offs because you knocked his team out of the running with your macho slide over home plate with a broken wrist. I think that's a pretty big 'F you' already."

"Nah, I gotta get him back better than that."

"And you're going to use me to do that."

"If you don't mind," he says with a charming smile, which will vanish when he learns Santino is becoming my cousin. It's such a swoon-worthy, forget-everything-else smile. I haven't seen it much in the last few days since… well, since *Santino* wrecked his wrist. And whatever else he seems to have on his mind that he won't tell me about.

"Come on," Cody says, turning toward the field. "No more procrastinating."

I trudge behind him. My mind flops back and forth between the impending tryouts and the impending wedding that will forever bond me to my best friend's nemesis. And then I realize Cody somehow weaseled out of telling me what's been bugging him. But, as he pointed out, I do have other things to deal with first.

I'd like to consider myself a dignified human being, but as we approach the field, I cower behind Cody's height. The team adores him. Maybe that adoration will transfer to me too.

"Cody," Chizz says when he sees us, "how many times do we have to go over this? *You* cannot try out."

"Yeah, man," Jiro says, patting his mitt. "We know you could own us, even with a fractured wrist, but give someone else a chance, for God's sake."

"As a matter of fact, that's exactly what I'm doing," Cody says. He steps aside, making it impossible for me to hide.

"Marnie," Chizz says, a note of surprise in his voice.

All eyes are on me. Then on the mitt on my hand.

"Hell. No," Joey says. He backhands Cody's arm. "The hell did you bring her here for?"

I intend to tell Joey to eat shit, but two menacing black

demon eyes are trained on me like a wildcat's readying for the kill. They belong to a tanned, muscular, six-foot-three body that goes by the name of Ray Torres. He's not glaring *per se*, but his frown looks like it's been drawn on with permanent marker, and his furrowed eyebrows scare the snark right off my tongue. Did I mention the menacing black demon eyes?

I've seen Ray from afar—in the hallway and at the one game he pitched when Cody had allergies so bad he couldn't stop sneezing. But up close, Ray looks like the Hulk, only less green and about a thousand times more angry.

"I came to watch," I squeak, and can hardly believe that *I*, a girl who prides herself in being confident and putting her money where her mouth is, have *squeaked* the most pathetic excuse ever.

Cody pushes me forward. "She came to try out."

I will punch him. I really will.

"I don't know if you know this," Ray says, "but you're a *girl*."

I can't find the badass in me to throw shade at him, but I manage to glare.

"Marnie, this true?" Chizz asks me.

"That I'm a girl?" I say. "Yes."

He frowns.

"Yes," I say, quieter. "I'm here to try out."

He studies me like he's performing a lie detector test. I expect him to laugh me off as a joke or tell me there's no way in hell I can try out. Instead he shrugs and goes, "Okay."

"*What?!*" Joey and Ray shout.

"Jiro, you're up first," Chizz says, ignoring them.

So that's it? He's not even going to question me about my decision? Have he and Cody been plotting this? Have I walked into their trap?

But you want this, Voice One in my head says.

At what cost? Voice Two in my head responds. *My dignity? My humility? Go home.*

And yet, my feet agree with Voice One. They walk me to the bullpen to warm up. My hands are getting clammy, and my nerves are tingling, sensations I haven't felt in a long time. These are pre-tryout jitters, pre-game jitters.

You've been through tryouts before. You've made it through *before*, Voice One says.

Voice Two: *That was* softball. *This is* baseball. *It's one thing to pitch with the guys at the sandlot, but you don't know all of these guys. Guys like Ray.*

Don't be a ninny, snaps Voice One.

Easier said than done. The team will watch my every move—they already are. And even if I'm not good enough to make the team, I've got to be good enough to prove that I have a reason to be here.

Or else you might as well walk into school naked tomorrow.

I step onto the practice mound, preparing for a pitch. But then someone steps between me and the pitching net on the other side of the bullpen, casting me in their looming shadow. Ray Torres.

"I was going to practice here," he says.

"Well…" I say slowly, subtly trying to locate the nearest bat. "I got here first."

He snarls. "Sorry, but my practice takes priority over you goofing around."

What a dick. "I'm here to try out too," I point out, even though he already knows this.

He scoffs. "That's funny. April Fools' Day was last month." He gestures toward the parking lot. "Go shopping. Get a makeover. The jock look doesn't suit you."

I stop looking for a bat and scowl at him. "Well, the asshole look doesn't quite suit you either, but hey, what are we gonna do? Now if you don't mind, I'd like to warm up."

His arms fall to his side as he pulls his shoulders back and juts out his chin. "You think we don't know that Cody's encouraging you so he can get in your pants?"

"You think I don't know that you're jealous that Cody's a

better pitcher than you and that he vouched for me instead of you?" Chills of terror and satisfaction flood me as fury flashes behind his eyes.

He lets out a menacing laugh, as if trying to prove my words mean nothing. "Whatever. Just try not to cry when you embarrass yourself, okay?"

He marches out of the bullpen, throwing an extra swagger in his step.

Controlling my rage, I watch as Ray passes Joey. Ray says something. Joey says something back. Then, as Ray walks away, Joey flips off the back of his head.

Looks like I'm not the only one who thinks Ray is an ass.

I focus on warming up. I throw a few easy pitches, not wanting to give away any of my special moves when I know the guys are watching.

And then, after what seems like two milliseconds, Chizz calls me over.

My heart starts pounding bass-drum thumps. Jiro, Ray, and the three other guys trying out watch me take the mound. Of them, only Jiro has a smile on his face. As much as I appreciate it, that is not enough to coax out my positive attitude.

"All right, Marnie," Chizz says, tossing a baseball to me. I'm so nervous, I'm surprised I don't drop it. "I'll tell you what I've told the others: I'm looking at your control, your speeds, your variation. Then I'll set up some defense plays to see you work in context, okay?"

I try swallowing, but my mouth is dry. I nod.

Chizz gives me a reassuring grin, and then he says quietly so only I can hear, "I'm rooting for you."

"You are?"

"I remember you used to watch Nick practice." He points to the dugout. "You sat right there and were always asking questions about pitching and strategy and technique. I used to think you were more invested in baseball than he was. And I've heard some interesting stories from your sandlot cohorts. I thought they were exaggerating, but if you've got the nerve to show up here, I can't help but think perhaps they weren't."

My first thought is to call bullshit. But if he wasn't rooting for me, why would he even let me waste his time?

"You've got the vote of the injured man himself," he reminds me.

Chizz is a coach. Part of his job is to give pep talks. But it's also to be honest. If you're doing something wrong, he's supposed to tell you and help you improve. So when Chizz tells me that he's rooting for me, there's a pretty high chance that he's got a reason to.

He moves back behind Davis, the catcher, this really

cool black guy who is so protective of home plate that last year for his birthday, Joey made fake adoption papers for Home Plate Keating, adopted son of Davis Keating. I take my place on the pitcher's mound. Standing next to Chizz, the assistant coach, Frankie, holds a radar gun to capture my speed.

I take a deep breath and position the ball in my hand for a curve ball. I dig the toe of my shoe into the sand and stand up straight. Shoulders back. No slouching. Elbow alignment. All things I learned in my previous softball life, reintroduced to me in Cody's Pitching 101 course.

I keep my eyes trained straight ahead. Cody is directly in my line of sight. He's watching me with all of Ray's intensity but none of his hatred. Cody subtly flashes me a sign: he makes a one with his right index finger.

Our sandlot code for a four-seam fastball.

Was I seeing things? Does he think this is my best pitch?

He gives me a slight nod.

I thought I'd start out with my curve ball, but when Cody flashes me the sign again, I change the position of my fingers on the ball. If he trusts me to take his spot, then I should trust him.

Heart pounding in my chest, I pivot my foot, bring my knee and arms up, take my stride, and—

The ball smacks into Davis's glove.

"Damn!" Frankie shouts as he reads at the screen of the radar gun.

I hold my breath.

"Eighty-four!" Frankie cries, which elicits a few more *damn*s from the sidelines.

Chizz grins like he's won the state title.

I knew I could throw fast, but never knew how fast. I mean, eighty-four. That's fast for a girl. And faster than average for a high school guy.

Damn.

I'm pretty good.

———

I don't consider myself a psychic, but when the phone rings at eight o'clock that night, I know it's Chizz.

Dad is the one who answers. "Hey, Jack. Long time no talk." And while they spend the next half hour catching up, I sit on the sofa, staring at—but not watching—the TV. My mind runs in circles: *He wants me to pitch. He doesn't want me to pitch. He wants me to pitch. He doesn't want me to pitch.*

Why would Chizz call at 8:00 p.m. to tell me that I didn't make the cut? Maybe he feels bad?

But deep in my gut, I know I made it.

I know because when I left the tryouts, I had that *feeling*.

I've spent the last three hours trying to figure out how I crushed the tryouts. Maybe it was my determination to spite Joey and Ray and the other doubters. Or maybe it was because once I threw that eighty-four-mile-per-hour pitch, my confidence came out of hiding. Whatever it was, I frigging *owned*.

What made the rest of tryouts easy was that during the mock defense plays, Chizz had Joey, Carrot, and Jiro all in the infield, so it was like playing at the sandlot. In fact, part of me thinks Chizz did that on purpose because he knows I play best with them.

He must really see something in me.

Either that or he's out of his frigging mind.

I'm trying to figure out which it is when Dad comes into the living room holding out the phone to me. "It's Coach Chizz."

I hesitate for a few seconds before taking it and putting it to my ear. "Hello?"

"Good news or bad news?" Chizz asks.

"Um. Bad news."

"Bad news is that we've got a few indignant players on the team," he says.

"Okay. And the good news?"

"Good news," he says, and I can hear the grin in his voice, "is it's because you're our new pitcher."

My mind goes blank. Is this *actually* good news, or have I voluntarily thrown myself into a shit storm?

Part of me wants to be proud of myself. The other part is already scared of stepping out on the field at the sectionals game. What comes out though is, "So it's legal that I can play on the guys' team?"

"Cleared it with the school board half an hour ago."

Shit. This is happening. I'm pitching for the guys' baseball team in the play-offs.

"Practice is at three forty-five tomorrow. Bring your mitt and cleats," Chizz says. "Oh, and congratulations."

8

I DON'T KNOW WHETHER TO CELEBRATE OR panic, but my dad is all for the former. As soon as he hears the news, the wine comes out. He's all like, "Can you imagine what it would be like if you won state? I mean, Nick going down in Corrington history is one thing, but both of you?" Then he starts imagining a local news story about us, and soon enough, the wine isn't enough. He whips out the frying pan and starts making dessert crêpes. This is the ultimate form of praise. Dad will cook you breakfast, lunch, or dinner, but if he's making you dessert, it means you're either graduating, getting promoted, getting married, or—the greatest achievement of all—pitching for the boys' baseball team.

Nick slaps me on the back with a quick "Congrats, Mini

Me," and then recaps the benefits of my accomplishments with underage sips of wine and a plateful of ice cream and crêpes covered in powdered sugar.

Mom offers me a smile, pours herself a small glass of wine, and then returns to her office to finish some work.

I eat my dessert, but the whole time I'm thinking, *What the hell have I done?*

———

No such celebration takes place at school, just whispers and rumors. It takes only one period for me to hear via Sara that Ray has been trash-talking me to anyone who will listen.

Which, apparently, is a lot of people.

I hear it first in the lunch line.

"My older brother, who knows a guy on the team, says the only reason she's on the team is 'cause her brother was some pitching god like three years ago, and the coach is pulling a Hail Mary hoping she's just as good."

"Samantha told me she screwed half the guys on the team to get picked."

"Maybe she had to screw the coach."

First of all, ew.

Second of all, *ew.*

"I'm standing right here, morons," I say. Their mouths

snap shut, and suddenly the floor becomes really interesting. It's as if they think I might bash their heads in with my tray. Part of me feels bad for scaring them, but then I remember what they said and add, "And just to set the story straight, I actually had to sacrifice the souls of all the guys on the team and drink their blood."

When I recount this to Sara at the lunch table, she says, "Focus on what's important: playing well, not stupid high school gossip. It's unavoidable and doesn't matter."

She's right, of course. It's not the student body I have to convince that I belong. It's the team. They're the ones I have to play with. They are the ones who have to trust me. Hopefully the guys' initial shock will wear off fast, and they'll objectively remember that I threw as well as any of the other guys at tryouts. Well, threw as well and better, if Chizz's choice reflects the truth.

In the meantime, I'll have to make sure I don't choke at the first practice. Owning at practice will show them that me owning tryouts was not a fluke.

Because it wasn't, I tell myself.

After school, I find myself stalling in the girls' locker room, taking my time French braiding my hair over my right shoulder and changing into my softball pants. Normally I'd join the other after-school sports girls in joking around, but I want to be alone.

I tie up my cleats and get nostalgic like I did this morning when I pulled them out of my closet. It was like bringing them back from the dead. *Hello, old friends.*

They're also a reminder of all the reasons I quit playing on an organized team in the first place.

With a deep breath, I grab my mitt. Time to go.

Outside, a cool breeze hits me. And so does Cody.

"Oh, hey, there you are," he says with a gentle slug to my shoulder. "I was looking for you. I thought you chickened out or something."

I look behind him for Sara, who said she would come watch practice.

"Sara had to go," Cody says, reading my mind.

"Where?"

"Emergency at the dog shelter. Moose escaped and took three accomplices with him. She had to split."

Normally I love hearing about the great adventures of Moose and Co., but today I couldn't be less interested.

"You're nervous," Cody says with an amused grin on his face.

"Why are you even here?" I ask. "Come to gloat? Tell me you were right?"

"I'm not Joey," he says. "Chizz asked me to be present for practice to talk you through some stuff, and anyway, I thought it wouldn't be so bad if I walked out there with you."

Thank God. But what I say is "I don't need a babysitter."

We stand there, me watching from afar as the team starts gathering on the field, trying to convince my feet to start moving. The sun peaks in and out between clouds, which means it shouldn't get in my eyes during practice. At least the weather is in my favor.

"You know, you don't have to pretend you've got all your shit together," he says. "At least not with me."

"I'm not pretending."

"Then how come you're still standing here?"

"Because I'm…" *Nervous as hell. Afraid of fucking up. Desperate for approval.* "I'm fine."

"It's okay to be scared. And it's okay to say that."

I'm not ready to say it out loud, but he gets my silence. When I don't reply, he gives my braid a gentle tug. "You've got this. Come on. Before they start thinking you're AWOL."

We start walking, and I have an overwhelming urge to cling to his right arm, like he's a lifeboat as the current is pulling me into a tidal wave. But I refrain. The game is in three days. I can't afford a lifeboat. I need to trust my ability to swim.

My old softball coach used to say, "Ten percent game, ninety percent brain." So I tell my nerves to get lost.

The guys are gathered on the infield—all wearing the same light gray baseball pants and their gym shirts. They slowly turn their attention toward me as I approach. Let me tell you, it is intimidating to have fifteen tall, muscular, testosterone-y (and okay, yes, *attractive)* guys staring me down like I'm a rabbit wandering into their wolf den. Forget the fact that I know some of them. Standing in a pack like this, I feel like I'm about to get eaten alive.

Then I spot Chizz, who will eat them if they try to eat me.

I don't have to decide whether to keep to myself or try to be friendly because Chizz is quick to put us all to work. He makes us run warm-up laps, and then he throws me in the bullpen with Davis and Cody so I can learn their signs.

Davis launches in. "So what exactly are your credentials?"

"I didn't know this was a job interview," I say. "Would you like me to print you a résumé and cover letter?" Beside me, Cody stifles a laugh.

"Who taught you how to pitch?" Davis asks.

He's on a mission for a serious answer, so I say, "My brother, my softball coach, YouTube." And then as an afterthought, I point at Cody and add, "Also, this guy."

"So you've never had a real pitching coach?" Davis asks skeptically.

"Well, my brother is Nick Locke," I remind him, hoping this will win me some points, but Davis says, "Yeah, so you better be *real* good."

Instead of gaining his confidence, I've raised his expectations. *Good job, Marnie.*

"Man," Davis says, stepping into the bullpen. "I remember watching that state game freshman year. That last inning…" He grins at the memory.

I know exactly what he's talking about.

In the top of the seventh, the score was three to three. This guy Zak was up at bat, and Jiro, who was a freshman then, was on second. There were two outs. Zak hit a line drive straight between right and center field. He made it to first, and Jiro was going for the double—going home. And then the worst thing that can happen to a runner happened: he got stuck in a rundown between third and home. The third baseman, the shortstop, the pitcher, and the catcher were all on him, but Jiro is a frigging cheetah on two legs. He was weaving in and out, back and forth—at one point, the third baseman and the shortstop collided trying to get him, and by some miracle, Jiro made it home safe.

So, it was up to Nick to defend the team's one-run lead in the bottom of the seventh. The first two batters made it on base before there were any outs. The crowd thought Nick was choking. The third guy hit a pop-up that was nearly a home run, but this kid Drew caught the ball with a flying leap. Then Nick struck out the last two batters.

It was epic.

And now Davis is going to expect me to live up to that. If only.

I listen intently as Cody and Davis explain their signal system to me. They have three different systems that they cycle through during a game. When they're finished explaining, they make me repeat it all, like, ten times to make sure I got it.

And then we start the real work: the pitching.

This part isn't so bad. It's like tryouts. I just have to throw my best, let Davis know he can trust me, and let him learn how I pitch and where those pitches land. He catches on quick. Cody throws in a few tips to fix the so-called "bad habits" I've picked up over the years.

When Chizz calls us back to the field so we can do some full-team drills, Davis seems neither disappointed nor impressed. He walks out of the bullpen without a word to me.

I pull off my mitt and shake out my hand. "He hates me."

Cody laughs. "Nah. He doesn't want to get his hopes up."

"What's it gonna take for them to like me?"

"Since when have you cared if people like you or not?"

"It may have been a while, but I haven't forgotten what it's like to be on a team. It's not enough if everyone is good on their own. You have to be good together. And that only works when you trust each other and when you like each other. With me on the team, neither of those conditions is met."

"You're jumping to conclusions," Cody says. "Jiro and Carrot thought it was a great idea. And everyone else, like Joey, will learn to deal. He's not the best at coping, but he'll figure it out. In time."

"We don't have time," I say. "We're T minus three days away."

Cody plays with the end of my braid, which he seems to be doing a lot this afternoon. "I think you're a lot more likable than you think you are."

I look up to meet his gaze. As always, I'm surprised at how tall he is, and I'm tall for a girl. The sun hits his face, making his eyes that light brownish-orange color with streaks of gold.

Damn. He could hypnotize a person with those eyes.

Or maybe I'm just a sucker.

After Chizz confirms that Cody has passed on our signals to me, he dismisses Cody, who decides to hang out with Sara and the dogs. As I join the guys around Chizz home plate, I force myself to focus. That seems to get harder and harder when Cody is around. I don't have the capacity to deal with him *and* pitching.

"Have you given him what he wants yet?" Ray hisses in my ear, snapping me out of my thoughts.

I instinctively take a step back from him. "What?"

"You and Kinski? He got you your spot. You do him yet?"

"Fuck off."

He snickers. "Don't think we all didn't see you having eye-sex with each other just now."

I take back my theory about teamwork. Maybe you don't have to like *everyone*. How can the other guys put up with him?

"You're an ass," I tell him. I step away from him, crossing my arms, pretending to focus really hard on what Chizz is saying.

The next part of practice involves me pitching to the guys. I knew this was coming, but it's no less daunting. But this is my chance to show them my game. It's one thing to have seen me pitch at tryouts. It's another to experience what my arm can do firsthand. Like Cody said, I'm not one to give up a chance to show up a bunch of guys.

Chizz splits up the fourteen players, putting seven in the field behind me, Davis behind home, me on the mound, and the rest in the batting lineup.

I throw some pretty good strikeouts, but one of them was against Carrot, so I have a suspicion that he let it happen.

With ten minutes left to practice, Ray the Menace is up at bat. He's been in the field, so this is my first time pitching against him, and he's the last person I want to get a hit. I don't even want him to make contact with the ball. I'm so intent on making sure this doesn't happen that I wind up throwing three balls. One more and he walks to first. That would be as embarrassing as if I let him get a hit.

On the fourth pitch, he smacks it clear over the fence.

A home run.

Shit.

Ray runs the bases, and when he gets home, he's not smiling triumphantly or gloating. No, he's scowling so hard, his face might permanently get stuck like that. His message is clear. *You suck, and I want you off my team.*

I don't even get a chance to redeem myself because Chizz calls the end of practice. The guys start gathering the equipment up to take back inside. I try to scout out Carrot and Jiro, thinking at least they will offer me positive words. But it's like they've forgotten I'm here, already on their way back to the locker rooms without even a glance my way. I'm about to call to them when someone snarls in my ear, "I wouldn't get too comfy with Cody. I don't think he'll be happy with you defiling his position."

It's my pal, Ray.

My hand clenches so tight I almost draw blood from my palm.

"Better get your shit together, *Locke*," he says. "We do this all over again tomorrow." And then he jogs ahead to catch up with the others.

Literally everything about him—his voice and face and

shitty attitude—boils my blood. I forget about seeking out my sandlot friends. All I want to do is get my hands around Ray's neck and squeeze until his face turns purple. And here I thought it wasn't possible for anyone to hate a person more than Cody hates Santino.

Chizz and I are the last two on the field. He comes up to me and says, "You were a trooper."

"I sucked," I say, defeated.

He laughs. "Nah, you didn't. You'll get into a groove."

"They think I sucked."

"Hey, I saw what you did out there today. And yesterday," Chizz says. "You've got it in you. You just play well and play smart and keep your chin up, and soon enough they'll see you've got a reason to."

"By soon enough do you mean in the next three days?" I ask. "Because that's really all the time I've got."

"A lot can happen in three days."

Yeah, right. Three days is nothing. Three days is like three seconds.

"Now get out of here," Chizz says. "Go home. Tomorrow is another practice."

I nod and trudge back to the girls' locker room, where I find a few softball girls are closing up their lockers. I used to hide from them, too embarrassed about quitting to face them. Now we'll say hi and exchange smiles, but it'll never be like it used to. No more joking around, no more after practice fro-yo trips.

"Marnie!" Carlie Burns shouts across the locker room. She's a senior and now the captain of the softball team. "We saw you pitching today! Lookin' good!"

"Oh…" I say. "Thanks." I'm afraid someone will make things awkward by asking why I won't pitch for them, but I'll pitch for the guys.

"Yeah," Carlie says, "Coach moved our practice to Saturday so we could see the game. Can't wait to see you kick some ass!" Her friends, some underclassmen I don't recognize, chime in their agreements, and then they grab their duffel bags and head out, leaving me alone.

I change fast into my street clothes and get the hell out. As I make it to the parking lot, I see the guys piling into cars. I catch up to Jiro.

"Are you walking home?" I ask, hoping to have some company.

"Nah, we're hitting Cecil's Grill House," he says.

"Oh…"

"Hey!" he shouts to the other guys. "Who's giving me a lift?"

"I got you, bro!" Joey opens the driver side door of his car.

"Cool!" I half expect him to ask if I want to come too, but he only waves and says, "See you!"

Soon they're all in their vehicles, zooming out of the parking lot. For a brief second, I catch Joey's eyes as he drives past me. It would be too much to expect *him* to invite me.

So I'm left standing there all alone.

I wish I could say that I can do perfectly fine without their approval or friendship or even acknowledgment. But damn. It hurts to be shunned.

9

WHEN MY MOM IS MAD, SHE NITPICKS EVERY little thing. Once, Nick forgot to close the garage door when he came home from hanging out with his friends, and my mom's bike got stolen. For days, all she did was criticize every last move any of us made. My hair wasn't combed. There were breadcrumbs on the table. The TV was too loud. Dad's footsteps were too clunky. Someone put a fork back with spoons.

So when I come home to her nagging Nick for not putting the car keys back in the key dish, I know one of us—me, Dad, or Nick—has done something wrong.

It makes me want to do a U-turn. But where would I go? The dog shelter? Sandlot? Sara's or Cody's? Not that I have time. I'm already in the kitchen. Mom's attention turns to me. "Marnie, how come you haven't gotten a dress for Abram's wedding like I asked you?"

I make myself look super exhausted from practice, so maybe she'll take some pity on me, but no such luck.

"Why is this so hard for you?" Her hair is in a messy bun, another sign she's wound real tight. "It's not like I'm asking you to pick a college."

Burn. Another task I've been avoiding, which has been ticking her off lately.

"I've got time," I say.

"For the dress or for college?" she asks. "Because as far as I can see, both are coming up real fast."

Okay, yes, the wedding is around the corner, but college applications don't need to be done until the end of this year.

Nick, who's sitting at the kitchen table, throws me a look like, *Thanks a lot.*

"How do you know I haven't gotten my dress?" I ask her, dropping my backpack under the island counter.

"You'd better not leave that there," she says. "And I checked your closet."

"I'll get it done," I mutter as I pick up my backpack and slip past her.

When I get up to my room, I'm greeted by a stack of college mail spread across my bed. Brightly colored envelopes with university logos scream, "Discover yourself!"

and "Say yes to success!" and "We want you!" No doubt Mom laid them out so I wouldn't miss them.

Nick had no problem getting into college. No problem with the transition to college. He was Ready with a capital *R*. He was ready to put away his cleats, ready to pack up his shit, and ready to move into Northwestern's dorms. He made peace with the fact that he wouldn't be seeing his high school friends every day. He and his girlfriend of three years had the smoothest breakup known to mankind. The fall of his freshman year, he left our small suburban town with all his loose ends tied up, ready to study computer science.

I've still got a year to go before it's my turn, but I can't imagine I'll be nearly as ready as he was. The thought of being away from home, the sandlot, and my friends makes my stomach knot. By now I should be getting sick of our baseball gang, sick of spending weekend after weekend throwing a ball around. Getting away from parents and starting fresh are what all the other juniors are talking about.

I scoop up the envelopes and shove them in the bottom drawer of my desk with the rest of their despicable brethren. Normally our family eats dinner together, but with mom aggravated with me, I think tonight we're each on our own for food, so I pull out my emergency stash of granola bars, crackers, and dried fruit, and then I surf the vast ocean of the internet for pitching videos.

I'm not normally one to spend hours on my computer, but I end up in a YouTube spiral, starting with videos of female baseball pitchers, to videos of Little Leaguers face-planting at home plate, to videos of successful sidearm and underhand pitchers.

That's when the most brilliantly stupid idea plants itself in my brain.

It's such a horribly genius plan that I shut my laptop, grab my wallet, and head downstairs before I change my mind.

"Going to Sara's house," I tell Mom, who's now on the phone and absently waves her acknowledgment at me.

I fish the car keys out of the key dish and fetch my mitt. Then I drive to Uncle Abram's house.

───────

Most sidearm and submarine pitchers aren't starters. They're usually reliefs. The coach starts off by putting an overhand pitcher on the mound, and then when he gets tired, the sidearm or underhand pitcher goes in. Their unique throwing style throws the batter for a loop. Sure, the batters might catch on after a few times at bat, but for the span of an entire lineup, the pitcher's got the upper hand.

It's not like a person can learn an entire style of pitching overnight, but I've got years of underhand pitching experience thanks to softball. And I probably wouldn't have thought about this plan if I didn't know someone who could teach me how to pitch underhand and/or side-arm for baseball. Except I happen to know someone who's caught the eyes of college scouts for his mad sidearm pitching style: Santino.

Abram's house is in a pretty classy neighborhood. I'm talking three-story houses, not including the basement, with huge-ass chandeliers that make you feel like you should be on the *Titanic*. Think five bedrooms, a trillion bathrooms, and pieces of furniture you can't touch because they might break if you look at them the wrong way.

Abram used to live in this house alone. Why he needed or wanted such a big house, I have no idea, presumably for all the art he collects. Or because he's a designer and needed a giant, well-designed house to show clients. Or because he simply likes to feel like a king.

So, when I pull up his ridiculously long brick driveway and there are two unfamiliar cars in addition to his silver sedan, I already feel like I'm in the wrong place.

When I ring the doorbell, Santino Acardi answers the door. He raises an eyebrow, clearly confused at my pres-ence and unsure of how to act after our last meeting went so badly.

He steps aside to let me in and then shouts, "Marnie's

here!" at the top of his lungs, like Nick and I do in our own home. It's unsettling that Santino acts like Abram's house is his house. There's this cognitive dissonance between him being the resident baseball field asshole and him living *here*. It's as if he's phased into two separate beings: Santino-the-Enemy, and Santino-My-Cousin. I can't reconcile them.

Abram comes down and meets us in the kitchen. He plops into a chair. "Marnie, Marnie, Marnie. This is a first—you coming out here on your own. You must be running away from home," he jokes.

"If I was running away from home, I wouldn't go to someone who would immediately call my parents," I say.

Down the hall, a toilet flushes. I expect Geanna to come out in some super formal outfit because she strikes me as the kind of person who would wear super formal clothes even when she's chilling at home.

Instead, a girl about my age with light brown skin and big brown eyes and long black hair comes out, wiping her hands on her ripped skinny jeans.

"Hi," she says when she sees me. She smiles wide, like she's in a commercial for toothpaste.

"Hi."

"Uh, Neha, this is Marnie," Santino says. "My…future… cousin. Marnie, this is my girlfriend, Neha." He sounds reluctant to introduce us, like he doesn't want me anywhere near his significant other. Like I might rip out her throat to avenge Cody.

"Hi, Marnie," Neha says, still smiling. "Nice to meet you. Santino and Abram have told me a lot about you."

If they have, why *is she smiling?*

"Don't be alarmed," Neha says. "I have no qualms about you being Cody's friend. Anyway, I think he sounds a lot like Santino, and if you want to *really* know the truth, I think Santino *loooves* Cody, which is why he appears to resent him so much. Denial. It's common among those experiencing unrequited *loooove.*" She jabs his stomach playfully, and he swats her hand away. If anyone else had put the words *Santino, love,* and *Cody* in a sentence, they'd have their tongues ripped out. But Santino laughs when she says it.

"Ignore her," Santino says. "Sometimes she strings words together that she thinks make sense." He tickles her side, making her squirm and giggle. I don't know whether to be disgusted by this overdose of cuteness or just plain confused. More cognitive dissonance.

Abram grins at me. "Told you she was a riot." For sure she is. Anyone who can turn Santino Acardi into a love-sick teenager can't be anything else.

Abram folds his hands behind his head and leans back in the chair. "So tell me. What brings you here without parental supervision?"

I glance at Santino.

"Him?" Abram asks.

I nod.

"You've come to turn my insides out?" Santino asks.

"Only if you don't do what I ask."

"Damn," Neha says. "No wonder he's scared of you."

The corner of my mouth quirks up.

"What do you want?" Santino asks.

"Teach me some of your pitching tricks."

He crosses his arms. "First your team knocks my team out of the play-offs, and now you want to steal my moves? Are you planning on selling them to your coach?"

"Not steal…" I say. "Borrow. And no, I'm not going to sell them. I'm going to use them."

He narrows his eyes suspiciously. "For what?" So he hasn't heard who Cody's replacement is. I guess he doesn't really care, now that baseball season is over for him.

"It's a long story," I say.

"I've got time."

At least he's willing to hear me out. It's more than I could have hoped for. I sit down next to Abram and gesture for Santino and Neha to take a seat as well.

"This is gonna be good," Neha says. "Is this a popcorn and Coke story?"

"Good idea," Abram says, getting up, presumably to

get the snacks. But I point at his seat so he'll sit back down. I don't have time for popcorn and Coke. I need pitching help.

So I tell them. Everything. From Santino benching Cody to me totally sucking ass at the softball sectionals two years ago to trying out for the baseball team to the guys resenting me.

After I finish, Santino leans back in his seat, mulling my story over. "And what do you think me teaching you is gonna do?"

"It will give me something new and different," I say. "I've had years of experience pitching underhand. If I could use that somehow to my advantage…"

"Pitching underhand softball is different than what I do."

"But it's similar. If I can get a handle on a good sidearm or underhand pitch for baseball, it's one more weapon in my arsenal."

"Why don't you ask Kinski?"

"Because (a) he only pitches overhand, and (b) if I need to remind you *again*, he's injured, because of you."

"Okay, could you nix it on the guilt trip?" he snaps. "I didn't do it on purpose."

"Yeah, okay, and I ate eighty-seven unicorns yesterday."

Neha and Abram both laugh.

"I'm not gonna help you if you're gonna be an ass about

it." He looks at Abram and goes, "Sorry," like Abram might care that he said *ass*.

"Well, are you in or not?" I ask.

Santino looks at me, then at Neha, then at Abram, then back at me. If he knew how much Cody would hate me even *talking* to him, Santino would probably say yes just to piss Cody off.

Speaking of which, this is going to piss Cody off.

Which is one more reason that telling him that Santino is going to be my cousin is going to be the hardest thing I've done all year, save for playing at sectionals.

"Fine," Santino says. "On one condition."

I frown at him.

"You stop being an ass."

I chew on the inside of my cheek so I don't say anything worth regretting. Then I opt for the mature response. "Fine."

The things I do for baseball.

———

I'm going to burn in hell for betraying my best friend.

Santino is a good pitcher. And he's a good teacher. He's actually helping me. And I'm letting him help me. I *asked* him to help me.

And that's not even the worst part. He's actually a decent human being.

Here, in his natural habitat, in the backyard of his new house with his girlfriend, Santino Acardi is not the biggest scumbag to ever walk the planet. It's almost impossible to think that *this* guy—who loves joking around with Neha and making her laugh—*this* guy cannot be the same person who fractured Cody's ulna with a ninety-mile-per-hour pitch. I mean, *shit*, *man*, Santino and Neha are frigging *cute*.

God.

Cute.

Sleeping puppies and face-planting penguins are cute. Not Santino Acardi and his girlfriend. At least, they're not supposed to be.

He opens doors for her. He gets her lemonade when she says she's thirsty. And she's always going out of her way to make him laugh.

If I wasn't so jealous of their seemingly perfect, stupid, *cute* relationship, I'd be absolutely disgusted.

I almost take a picture of them to send to Cody and Sara and Joey because this is an anomaly only they would understand, but then I'd have to explain why I'm witnessing this lovefest in the first place.

And when Santino's not being one half of the perfect couple, he's spewing out pitching tips—how to convert my underhand to a sidearm, how to control a sidearm pitch to stay in the strike zone. He even has an entire folder of sidearm pitching videos bookmarked on his computer. He shows me the footage he's slowed down using some movie editing software. He has sidearm pitching down to a science, and he shares it all with me.

"This is the part where you're supposed to say 'thank you,'" Santino says as we go back inside after what seems like an entire week's worth of pitching camp.

I don't know if I'm ready to say "thank you" to the person who has been a pain in my best friend's ass for the last three years, but he did genuinely help me, so I compromise and say, "Thanks," to please him for a moment, and then I add, "for hitting Cody in the arm and causing all of this madness to happen in the first place."

"Ah-ah. Not being an ass was part of the deal," he says. He grabs bottles of water from the fridge for each of us.

"To be fair," Neha says to him, "it *is* kind of your fault."

"Hey, whose side are you on?" he teases.

She puts her hands up like she's innocent. "I shall be Switzerland." Then she mouths at me, "Your side."

Santino shakes his head at her and says to me, "Fine, hold a grudge if you want, but I could give you some pointers for how to take advantage of the North Enders at sectionals. I've got a"—he pauses—"*former* friend on the team, and I used to watch him play a lot. I know their lineup like nobody's business."

I narrow my eyes at him. "And what would you like in return?"

"For you to kick their asses."

"Really? Between us and the North Enders, you'd rather have *us* win? *Cody Kinski's* team?"

He hesitates as he takes in my point and then nods. "Okay, fine. I really couldn't care less who wins." He shrugs. "I don't want anything in return."

"How do I know that in five years, you won't come to me one day and be like, 'Hey, remember that time I gave you all my pitching secrets?' and then ask me for two hundred bucks?"

He laughs. "I'm trusting that this wasn't all a hoax for Kinski to steal my moves next year. So you gotta trust me in return." He chugs a fourth of his water bottle.

We're silent for a moment, and I think this might be a truce proposition. Perhaps even an offer of, dare I say, friendship?

"By the way," Santino says, "how did the bastard react when he found out his best friend is going to be cousins with his mortal enemy?"

I want to give him shit for calling Cody a bastard—takes one to know one, that kind of jab—but the fact Santino assumes that I've already told Cody the news is a sucker punch. *I still haven't told him.*

And for what? I keep telling myself I don't want to make him any more miserable. Which may or may not be what happens. But either way, Santino is going to be my cousin, and I came to him for pitching help. I mean, Cody doesn't have a say in who I hang out with or who I ask for pitching tips, but we're friends. I owe him my honesty. I tell him everything. Except, maybe, for how much I like to be around him and stare at his stupid, attractive face. And apparently about all the interactions I've had with Santino in the last week.

Perhaps, in a surprising turn of events, *I* am the biggest scumbag to walk the planet.

"I take it from your silence that you have not told him," Santino says.

"Are you guys in a relationship?" Neha asks. "Romantically, I mean?"

"No," I say. "But I have a feeling there will not be a relationship of any kind when he finds out what a traitor I am."

Santino nods slowly, as if he's finally understanding why I'm having trouble being nice to him.

"You know, I'm probably not as bad as he paints me out to be," he says. As an afterthought, he adds, "And he's probably not as bad as I paint him out to be."

"That tends to be the way it is with people you don't like," Neha says.

As I talk with the two of them, calling a truce seems so simple. But it's painful to think how it would kill Cody— and Joey and Carrot and Jiro and Sara, for that matter. I might as well stick knives in their stomachs.

"If it makes you any happier," Santino says, leaning back in his chair, "I'm not too thrilled about the situation, either. But for different reasons than you."

"What do you mean?"

He shrugs as he spins the cap of his water bottle on the table. "How would you like it if your supposedly responsible mom got knocked up by some guy she's only been dating for a little while? And then they decide to get hitched as soon as possible?"

Suddenly, the house isn't big enough. What if Abram or Geanna hear him saying these things?

"You don't want your mom to get married?" I ask, feeling like I've been told top secret CIA information.

"Sure. One day. But not like this."

"Do you even like Abram?" I'm not sure I want to know the answer.

"I hardly know the guy. Sure, he's nice, pretty chill. He knows jack shit about baseball, but he plays video games with me. He's trying. And he makes my mom happy. He's the only person who can get her head out of her work. But it's real fast."

I can't believe I'm having this conversation with Santino. Has he told anyone else how he feels about this marriage besides Neha?

"Do you want to be an older brother?" I ask him.

Before today, the thought of anyone having Santino for an older brother would scare the hell out of me for that person. I mean, he hit a dude with a baseball. How older brotherly could he be? But after seeing Santino off the field, seeing him as an actual human being…I feel kind of bad for him.

Santino grabs Neha's hand and absently plays with the rings on her fingers. "I don't know. I'll only be here for another year or so before I start college."

"So where is your dad in all this?" I ask.

"Don't know. Don't really care, either. He left my mom right after I was born. Supposedly he's married and has another family now. Doesn't want anything to do with us. But I'm okay with that. My mom and I have gotten along just fine without him. It actually feels weird that our family is going to be twice as big."

Suddenly a desperate need to get out overwhelms me. I don't want to hear this. I don't want to know about Santino's past. I don't want to see him doting on his girlfriend. All of that will make it ten times harder to tell Cody the truth.

I make up some excuse about getting home. I find Abram and Geanna to say goodbye, then Neha and Santino walk me to the car.

As I'm about to close the door, Santino says, "Listen, I might not be the most decent person on the field, but you should know that family is the most important thing to me."

I nod then give a final wave and start the car. Family is important to me too, and that includes my sandlot family. I only wish it didn't feel like my two families were on opposing teams. I'm a pitcher, not a referee.

10

IF IT HASN'T BEEN SCIENTIFICALLY PROVEN that adorable puppies make everything better, then I can provide the anecdotal evidence. Something about the little fur balls makes life's stresses seem less daunting. Maybe it's that musky dog smell or the abundance of wagging tails. All I know is that when I get overloaded with cute, the storms inside me subside.

So when I step into Fox & Hound Rescue to pick up Sara for school, and Moose, the two-year-old border collie mix, comes out from behind the reception desk to greet me, I can't help but smile.

"Hello, Moose," I say, scratching behind his ears. "I heard you got up to some trouble." I pat his head. "Go find Sara."

This is a command he knows well. He trots off through the doorway to the back of the shelter where the kennels are.

Moose is the only dog they let run loose in the shelter. He's Sara's favorite. I think she wants to keep him, but her mom won't let her because they already have three dogs.

Usually Sara's ready to go, as she hates to be late. So when I'm still standing at the front desk five minutes later, I decide to go back and see what's taking so long.

What I stumble upon is an argument.

I lurk outside the kennel where dogs yip over Sara and her mom's bickering.

"I don't want to leave them," Sara says with frustration. "They're my best friends. This is what I want to do. This is where I want to be." I've hardly ever heard Sara get frustrated, which is saying something, seeing as I've known her since I was six years old.

"You need to go to college, Sara," Camilla says. "I'm not going to let your future go to the dogs. Literally."

"But who will help run the rescue when I'm at college? You're always busy with all the design work for Mr. Dickwad—"

"Mr. Dickson," Camilla corrects her. "And there are the other volunteers who will be around."

"But I *love* the dogs. I want to help them find homes."

"There will be other people to help them find homes.

We've already got the majority of our dogs in foster homes. Soon we won't even need this kennel."

"But we *do* need the kennel, for all the dogs that don't get fostered. And I *like* it here."

"Yes, but, Sara, this is not a full-time gig. You need to go to college so you can get a job and make money, and then you can spend all the time you want here."

Wait, what? Sara doesn't want to go to college? Like, at all? I mean, I don't want to go to college *now*, but I know I will eventually. I'm so preoccupied trying to process all this that by the time I hear footsteps coming out the door, it's too late.

Sara emerges from the kennel and runs straight into me before I can even pretend that I just arrived. Moose is at her heels.

"What are you doing?" Sara demands.

"Sorry…I was…" There is no way to get around the fact that I was eavesdropping. "I was looking for you."

"Sara, we're not done—" Camilla shuts up as soon as she sees me. "Oh, hey, Marnie, how's it going?" Normally, she's the type of person who actually wants to know how it's going and will pull you into conversation for half an hour. But I can tell from her tone that she's out of sorts and doesn't care how I'm doing.

"Hi." I point to the door. "If it's a bad time…"

"Nope, you're just in time," Sara says. "Otherwise we'll be late for school."

We won't be anywhere near late, but I don't say anything. Sara slings her backpack over her shoulder and heads toward the door. "Don't forget that family is coming to check Maple out later today," she says to her mom curtly, meaning she's done arguing. For now.

I keep my mouth shut on the drive to school even though I'm bursting with a million questions. But she deserves the chance to yell at me for being a snoop before I get to ask any questions.

When we're halfway to school, she starts talking.

"What's wrong with wanting to take care of dogs?" she asks. "I like dogs. Dogs like me. Seems like an ideal situation, right?"

"I didn't know you didn't want to go to college," I say, now that I know the topic is open for conversation.

"I've only recently started thinking about it."

Me too, I want to say, but this isn't about me. "Well, your mom's right," I say instead. "You do need a way to make money."

"I know." She sighs. "But there are other ways to do that than going to college—dude. Dude! *Yellow light*."

I slow to a stop. I don't know what to say to her. Considering I've given college about zero thoughts, it's not like I have a lot of advice. I mean, lots of kids in our class seem ready to move on, but I like my home. I'm not itching to change how things are—and figuring out what I want a year from now? Two years? The rest of my life? That shit is too far for me to see, and I've got nearly 20/20 vision.

"And I don't know," Sara continues, "I love it here. I could spend the rest of my life in this town and be perfectly happy. I mean, yeah, my mom and I disagree on certain things, but we're all each other has. And our house is close to everything. It's clean. Low crime rate. It's perfect. And I can't stand the thought of being away from the dogs for four years while I'm at college."

"You can always go to a college in state so you can come home on the weekends," I offer.

She sighs. "It's not the same."

The light turns green. "I guess I don't really understand since I've never had a pet," I say.

"You have *no* idea," she says. "You've never had a pet, *and* you've got a whole family."

I don't immediately see how these points are related. Sara's dad died of a heart attack when she was three, so she doesn't really remember him. Hence, she doesn't really miss him. At least, I didn't think she did. Every time he gets brought up, she seems completely indifferent.

"What do you mean?" I ask her.

"Well, you've got a mom, a dad, *and* a brother. And you've got a big extended family—which will get bigger when your uncle gets married. But me? It's always been me and my mom. She's an only child, all my grandparents are dead, and I hardly ever see relatives from my dad's side of the family. I've never minded that it's only the two of us, though. I mean, I've got you and Cody and Joey. And I've got my dogs."

My heart swells almost to the point of physical pain. I always knew that Sara had a small network of friends and family, but I never knew how small until she says it out loud.

I wish I had something deep to say. But "It'll all work out" or "You'll find a way" seem useless. I stay silent.

"It's okay," she says. "You don't have to say anything. It's hard."

"Yeah" is all I say.

I pull into the school parking lot. Some aggressive ass hats snag two prime parking spots before I grab one in the farthest part of the lot.

"Hey," Sara finally says as we get out of the car. "How was practice? I meant to text you about it."

"I would say pretty good. I'm sure you'll hear differently depending on who you ask." As we walk toward the entrance, I tell her about Ray. She offers to drop-kick him across the baseball field.

"Oh yeah," she says on our way to the library atrium, "and did you ever get that dress your mom was hounding on you to get?"

"Nope."

"Did you tell Cody about Santino?"

"Nope."

"You are winning at life right now."

I laugh, even though I know she's changing the subject to deflect from her problems. I guess that's part of the job description—be a distraction when your friend needs one.

"Are you planning on telling him anytime soon?" she asks.

I adjust my backpack on my shoulders. "Yeah. Soon." *Maybe.*

"He's going to find out eventually."

"I know."

"If this blows up in your face, I'm going to have to take Cody's side. You're sort of being a weasel about it."

Guilt stabs me as I think about yesterday. How I hung out with Santino and his girlfriend. How I actually started to befriend the asshole who injured Cody.

I need to air out my sins to someone, so I open my mouth to tell Sara everything, but then we see Joey near the front of the library, and he's too close for me to mention my pitching lesson with Santino.

I expect him to come over and give me shit after

yesterday's practice, but he gives us a strange look and hurries away. Or, rather, he gives *Sara* a strange look and scurries into the sea of students ahead of us.

I glance at Sara. "What was that?"

She avoids eye contact.

"Sara..."

"Don't worry about it."

"And what, exactly, is *it?*"

"Nothing," she mumbles and then heads to our atrium table.

Of course, this makes me worry about it or at least *wonder* about it. But I don't press her. Because there are some things you don't press Sara about, and one of those things is what the hell happened between her and Joey. Anyway, she's already had a tough morning with her mom. I don't want to put her on defense again.

I guess we're all entitled to have secrets, no matter how long we've known one another. God knows I've got a big one.

11

YESTERDAY NIGHT, WHEN I CONFESSED THAT I went to Santino for pitching help, Nick applauded me for thinking outside the box. "Show them what you learned," he said when I expressed worry about what my teammates would say. "What's the worst that could happen?"

"Uh, they hate me even more than they already do?"

"Look, you don't have to be Nolan Ryan to have earned a spot on the team. Save for a couple of the guys, even though it's varsity, baseball is probably not their priority. When I was on the team, it was either you were *really* into baseball—like Joey and Cody and the other guys you play with at the sandlot—or you liked the sport and thought it would look good on your college applications. High school ball isn't everything."

His advice made sense, but I had to adjust for bias. It was coming from him, who (1) played ball not really because he loved it but because he was too good not to play, and (2) has since graduated and can see all this stuff in hindsight.

So Nick hadn't quite eased my mind about going to practice. In fact, he made me realize how all of the guys on the team are *really* into baseball, because come to think of it, none of them seem like résumé-filler players. Like, they would all rather die than lose sectionals. Not to mention that, before Cody's injury, losing sectionals was never even a possibility. It was the semifinals they had to fret about. So, correction, they'd rather have *me* die than lose sectionals.

As murdering me would land them in prison for life, their next best option is to ignore me. But when you're playing on a team, and the performance of said team depends largely on how well its members communicate… well, neglect does more damage than good.

So, before practice starts, I go to someone who I know will offer me support.

"Chizz," I say.

He looks up from his clipboard of notes. "Marnie."

"What if I told you I could pitch sidearm?"

He raises an eyebrow, so I gesture at the bullpen. He follows me over, and I demonstrate what Santino taught me. How the ball approaches the plate from an odd angle.

How even though I may not be able to pitch as fast or with as much break with a sidearm pitch, the delivery in itself is tricky enough to deceive a batter who isn't used to it. Most high school players aren't, which is why Santino seems to be so successful. Or so Santino says.

Davis approaches, catcher gear in his arms. "What's going on?"

"Sidearm pitching is what's going on," Chizz says.

I inspect his face, trying to figure out what he's thinking. He stands with his hands on his hips and sucks on a tooth, which means he's thinking real hard. He hasn't said no, so I tell Davis my plan (*my* plan, I frame it), and then I show him what I mean.

Davis doesn't scoff like I expected him to. Instead, he gives what I think is a satisfied nod and goes, "Hm. Interesting. Two styles of pitching. Now that's something Nick Locke didn't do. Or Cody, for that matter."

I can't help but grin. Stepping out of Nick's and Cody's shadows is enough to replenish my well of confidence.

"You know," Chizz says after a really long silence, "I think it could work." My heartbeat skyrockets. "At least for a couple innings. Sure, batters might catch on, but the first time will throw them for a loop."

Davis nods in agreement as Chizz pats me on the back, congratulating me for bringing my brains to the game.

"I'm impressed," Davis says as we follow in Chizz's wake. The compliment gives my pride a boost.

Back on the field, Chizz shares the plan with the rest of the guys. His pep talk boosts my field cred, because when Chizz has me pitch to the guys, testing out my sidearm, none of them throw me any dirty looks. In fact, I'd almost go as far as to say they are intrigued, which is the first sign of interest (*good* interest) they've shown in me since I joined their team.

"Your sidearm plot. That's clever, Marnie," Jiro tells me after Chizz lets me take a breather. He doesn't want me to throw my arm out.

"Oh, now you're talking to me," I say, remembering how he left me hanging in the parking lot after last practice.

"What?" He offers me a drink from his water bottle, and I shake my head. "What do you mean?" he asks.

I sit down on the dugout bench next to him. "I hate to accuse you of being a bad friend, but you've kind of been a bad friend."

He throws his hand over his heart like I've shot him. "Explain yourself!"

"After Chizz put me in Cody's place, it's felt like you and Carrot and Joey have, I don't know…removed yourselves from me. I mean, I know Joey's pissed at me, but you and Carrot? I thought you'd guys at least spread the word that I'm not a *complete* waste of space."

Jiro bites his lip. "Well, we *did*. But…sometimes you can come off as a little…harsh."

"Harsh?"

"You've got a reputation for being, well, *you*."

"What's that supposed to mean?"

"Feisty. Selective in who you like and dislike. And sometimes you look kind of intimidating." He shrugs when my eyes bug out of their sockets. "I think you might have scared off some of the guys."

"*Me?*"

He laughs a little. "That, and also Ray has been trying to convince the guys you bribed Chizz into letting you on the team. With money, or…other things."

"*Ew.*" I shudder.

"Yeah, I know."

"*And—*"

"There's *more?*"

He nods. "Half the guys are afraid Cody will go ballistic if any of them get within five feet of you."

"Why?"

He gives me a knowing look. It takes me a moment.

Does every person on the planet think Cody is completely smitten with me? I don't see it. Maybe he's got a *crush*, but crushes are tiny. They go away.

"Cody isn't the jealous type," I say, not really knowing if this is the truth or not. It's not like I've ever went out with anyone to know how he would react. Or even had other guy friends besides him and Joey. Sure, there are Jiro and Carrot, but…

Have either of *them* ever wanted to ask me out but were too afraid that Cody would get pissed at them?

No.

This is dumb.

If Cody wanted to ask me out, he would've.

Right?

He's not a coward.

But then again, if he thinks about me even half as much as I think about him and does as much as I do about it (which is to say, nothing), maybe he is a coward.

Just like me.

Hell.

I don't have time to think about this.

"Cody thinks of you guys as his brothers," I say. "Except Ray maybe. He would never get mad at you guys for talking to me."

Jiro grins as he stands and stretches his arms. "That's exactly it. We're like his brothers. It's code to stay away from the girl he's—"

"Whatever," I interrupt, not wanting to hear what comes after that. *The girl he's got a crush on. The girl he's liked for the past who knows how many years. The girl he's in love with.*

Except he's not in love with me.

I don't want to know how he feels about me. Because then I'd have to sort out how I really feel about him. And I'm not ready for that.

I've got to focus on this game. I have to focus so I can win. To show Joey and Ray and the rest of the team that winning is possible, even with me on the team.

I also have to win this for Cody. This win belongs to him. He's worked hard all season, and I can't be the one to take that away from him.

"Chizz is calling us over," Jiro says, nodding back at the field. He holds out a bat. "I know you won't be batting at the game, but you should practice with us anyway."

I take the bat from him. I'm going to be here for the rest of practice, anyway, so I might as well join in on their batting drills. And I don't totally suck at batting, so it's another way to show them I know what I'm doing.

As I follow Jiro back to the field, I mull over everything he's told me—about how the guys are afraid of me and about how Ray is defaming me. And I think about Cody. Cody in his cast who is upset about more than not being able to play at sectionals game but won't tell me what.

In a way, they're one and the same—this game, Cody. I can't have one without the other.

As if he might materialize from my thoughts, I look

toward the bleachers where I imagine he's slipped in while I wasn't paying attention. To watch us. Watch me.

Maybe he's at home, wishing he was here, playing. Or maybe he's at the doctor's. Or plotting Santino's demise.

As I wait for my turn to bat, I try to focus on what's happening in front of me, but my mind keeps wandering, trying to plan what exactly I could say to Cody to tell him the news of Santino becoming my cousin without completely shattering his world, what I could say to explain how Santino might not be such a bad person without completely shattering our friendship.

"Marnie, you're up," Chizz says.

I push Cody out of my mind and step up to the plate, swinging the bat over my shoulder. Jiro, one of the team's relief pitchers, is standing on the mound. He winds up. I smack the ball between left and center field—an easy double.

I run to first as Ray jogs to second. There's time to take another base, so I keep on running after my foot hits the plate. On second base, Ray has his arms crossed lazily, his weight resting on one side of his body. *Why isn't he going to third?*

Normally, I would avoid shouting at Ray for fear of being buried alive, but out of instinct, as I'm running to second, I shout, "Go!"

He just stares at me, his shoulders relaxed, arms still crossed.

So I'm stuck between first and second as the ball is on its way back to first, where I'm going to get out if I don't get there first.

Silently cursing Ray, I change directions back to first, pumping my legs, taking the longest strides I can to beat the ball to the base—almost like Cody in the last play of the regionals game. But it's too late. The ball is already in Wes's hand. I'm out.

Chizz comes onto the infield. "What the hell was that?"

"Sorry," I mumble, even though it wasn't really my fault. "I thought—"

"Why didn't you run to third?" he asks. He's addressing Ray.

No one was talking before, but the field gets very quiet.

Ray, still standing on second base, acts bored, like he's waiting for a pot of water to boil, and shrugs. "There was no time."

"There was plenty of time," Chizz says, his voice stern.

"She's too slow," Ray says. "She would've gotten out anyway." He glances at his teammates, waiting for them to back up his statement. I sneak a glance at Joey. If we were at the sandlot, he'd launch the blame at me, because that's what Joey likes to do. But on this field, he doesn't say anything.

"No, she wouldn't have," Carrot says, from his place on

third. He gives me a slight nod. I get the feeling Jiro slipped in a word about how I've felt isolated.

A tense silence fills the air as Ray and Chizz stare each other down. It's like an icy wind has swept through, even though it's the end of May and the sun is beating down on us. I don't know what to do. Should I defend myself? I'm sure if I open my mouth, Ray will stuff me in a garbage can later.

"Marnie," Chizz says without looking at me. "Go pitch with Davis."

Davis and I exchange apprehensive looks but don't question Chizz.

Silently, I follow Davis to the bullpen as Chizz calls everyone else into a huddle—one that I don't need to be in but am probably the subject of.

"You know," Davis says. "If our team was a democracy, we'd have voted Ray off the island eons ago."

I do something I don't think I've done at practice yet—I smile. "Thanks."

"I'm glad you decided to try that sidearm trick," Davis says as we set up to practice my pitching. "It's pretty ingenious. I mean, throwing a girl into the equation and *then* adding your sidearm? That'll confuse the hell out of the other team."

At first, I'm suspicious of his kindness. Jiro didn't have

that much time to tell the guys how I was feeling. But they must be starting to understand, from watching me practice, that I'm not here for shits and giggles. I'm here to help them win. And dammit, we are going to win.

12

WHEN WE WERE KIDS, CODY AND I USED TO
have races around our subdivision. Back then, I actually had
a chance of beating him, what with both of us being short
and scrawny. Now, as I wait for Cody on his driveway in my
running shorts and my old softball T-shirt, I wonder how
fast he'd lose me if we raced today. He'd probably have my
pace doubled within the first two blocks. Even with his cast.

The front door opens, and Cody comes out in basketball shorts and his infamous black running tank. It's a faded
black shirt with the sleeves cut off, but the armholes are so
big I can see through to his chest and abs.

God damn.

I like to tell myself this view is not the reason I like
running with Cody more than Sara. And it's also not the

reason I'd rather run with him than by myself. I run with Cody because he's a better runner than me, better than Sara, and running with him challenges me to improve my pace. Or so I like to tell myself.

I bend down and pretend to tighten my shoelaces so he can't see my wandering eyes.

"Sure you can run with that?" I ask, standing and gesturing at his cast.

He nods.

"What did your doctor say about running with a cast?"

He shrugs.

"Cody Kinski, if you trip and face-plant and break the rest of the bones in your arm, I will not be held accountable."

"Noted," he says. He stretches his one good arm over his head, and the hem of his shirt lifts, revealing a sliver of skin.

I force myself to face down the street. "Let's go."

As always, I pick our route. Cody, who usually runs a few steps ahead of me, stays a few steps behind. Is he being deliberately slow to make me feel better about myself or is his wrist hurting him? I try asking him about it, but he says he's fine.

This is what we do sometimes—night runs, when the sidewalks are lit by the glow of streetlamps and the lights are on inside the houses we pass. Every once in a while, the whir of a car driving down a nearby street will reach us, but for the most part, it's quiet save for our footsteps on the pavement.

I suppose I also run with Cody because it's less lonely. And I feel safer, even though it's a quiet neighborhood, aside from the occasional aggressive dog.

We hardly ever talk when we run. It's a waste of oxygen. But it's enough to feel him nearby, hear his steady breathing. Normally I try to match my steps with his, match my breathing with his, but tonight, he's following my pace. His energy seems low, less driven than it usually is on our runs.

When I decide we've run long enough—a mile and a half, maybe two?—I start turning back toward our street.

Cody grabs my elbow and pulls me in the other direction. "Detour," he says.

"Whoa," I say, letting my momentum swing me around. "Detour where?"

He lets go of my arm and points. At first I think he's talking about the maple trees lining the other side of the street, but then he gestures at the lights a little farther down at Corrington Terrace, the outdoor mall a few blocks away.

"We're *running* there?" I ask. "Wasn't this long enough?"

"We were going slow," he says, a teasing jab at my pace. "And anyway, you've got to be in shape for the game."

"I *am* in shape," I say, following him as he jogs toward Corrington Terrace.

"Get in *more* shape," he says with a laugh.

Any other day, I'd tell him to go eat himself, then run back to my house as fast as I could before he could catch up, but maybe this is a chance to tell him that my uncle is going to marry Santino's mom. And that I've befriended Santino.

And maybe it's a chance to figure out what's bugging him.

So I run, and he lets me take the lead again. We run all the way to Corrington Terrace, where it's so lit up with florescent lights and storefront displays that it's like we've arrived in another dimension. People mill about, hanging out by the center fountain and having late dinners on the patios at the restaurants. It smells like baked pretzels, popcorn, and Chinese food. Our neighborhood a few blocks away is settling in for the night, but here, the nightlife is waking up.

"Don't tell me you're going to make me run stairs," I say, glancing at Samson's, which is a three-story department store that has the steepest flights of stairs known to humankind. Sara and I went there for a workout a few times. We got in a lot of exercise before we got kicked out.

"I actually had *that* in mind," he says, pointing to Walker's.

"Ice cream? Seriously? I thought I'm supposed to be getting in shape."

"You're already in shape," he says, mimicking me from earlier.

And since I'm not one to say no to ice cream, I follow him inside.

Walker's looks like an old-fashioned ice-cream parlor, with black-and-white-tiled floors, round white tables with white chairs, and a scene of a dairy farm wallpapered on the back wall. Old Mickey Walker with his white hair stands behind the freezer display with his forty-two different flavors of ice cream. There's a family with four kids, all reaching over to try one another's flavors. At another table in the corner, two guys hold hands, sharing a giant sundae.

Seeing them makes me wonder if this might be considered a date. Me and a very attractive guy who I may or may not *like* like, getting ice cream late at night. If anyone else had told me they were in such a situation, I'd say, yeah, that's a date.

But this isn't a date.

Because it's just Cody.

And we've done this before. So many times.

"How can I help you two?" Mickey asks us, scooper in hand.

Cody and I step up to the freezers and scan the options. I never feel more indecisive than when I'm at Walker's.

Cody has his order ready. He always gets the same thing: two scoops of black cherry and one scoop of cookie dough.

Me, on the other hand, I always feel like I need to try something new.

"You pick for me," I tell Cody.

"Just get your favorite," he says.

"I don't know what my favorite is."

"*I* know what your favorite is," he says.

"Of course you do."

He turns to Mickey, and I'm not sure what's going to come out of his mouth.

"Regular vanilla with dark chocolate fudge and sprinkles. The round ones, not the long ones."

I nod. Yeah, that *is* my favorite.

Mickey hands us our bowls, and Cody gives him a ten-dollar bill to cover both our orders. He doesn't usually have anything in his pockets when we run, which means he planned this.

As we head back outside and take a table under the red-and-white awning, I say, "You're going to let me pay you back for this, right?"

He shakes his head. "On me."

Is he trying to trick me into a date? Does *he* think it's a date? It can't be a date. We're in running clothes, both sweaty and probably smelly. And it's *us*. Joey and Sara have already proven that you don't fuck with your friendships, exhibited once again by their weird eye contact earlier today.

"So what's this all about?" I ask, hoping he will tell me if we're on a date right now.

He digs his spoon into his ice cream. "Carrot told me what happened at practice today. About Ray. And that apparently you can pitch sidearm?"

I nod.

"He said Chizz delivered a really angry speech too."

"About me?"

"About how the guys should treat you like you're one of them. And that Chizz said if any of them are mean to you again, he'll take them off the roster for sectionals."

"That seems harsh."

"Yeah, no one believed him," Cody says.

"Of course not. Chizz is a softy at heart. We all know it."

"Until Ray said…what did Carrot say? Right, that you were, quote, 'Whoring around with everyone to pitch.'"

My eyes bulge. "He said *what?*" My hands curl into fists.

Cody notices. "You don't have to declare war. Chizz followed through on his threat."

"He kicked Ray off the team?"

Cody nods.

"But Ray is one of our power hitters."

"Doesn't matter if he's an asshole."

I'm stunned into silence, in awe of Chizz's belief in me. Not just his belief, but his sense of justice. Giving up one of his best—albeit douchiest—players in favor of me? To preserve my dignity? Or maybe for the whole team's dignity. It might be the right thing to do, but it's still a gargantuan risk.

"Why's Ray so bitter anyway?" I ask. "He's a giant sack of anger management issues."

"When Nick graduated, Ray thought he was going to take his place. And he's a senior now, so it's his last chance to prove himself."

"But then you came along."

"Yeah. And then you, and his ego can't take being bested by a girl."

"Well, to be fair, sometimes neither can yours," I tease, pointing my spoon at him.

"Funny, I don't recall ever having been bested by a girl."

In retaliation, I lean over the table and swipe a spoonful of his ice cream.

"Spoons to yourself, woman!" he cries, pulling his bowl away from me.

He laughs, and for a moment, it's like he doesn't have a cast on his arm, like he's not crushed he won't be able to play in sectionals, like it's any other day, and the two of us can just be *us*. No confusion, no secrets.

"So where'd you learn to throw sidearm anyway?" Cody asks.

My heart lurches in my chest. He's literally asked the exact question that will lead me to tell him everything. All I have to do is answer truthfully.

Sounds so simple, and yet the next words that pop out of my mouth are, "I watched some YouTube videos." I look down at my ice cream. "Talked to Nick. Read up on it."

"Cool. I heard you were totally badass. That was smart." I still can't look at him. He lightly kicks my foot under the table. "Guess you're not as dumb as you look."

I. Am. Scum.

Scum squared.

Next to his bowl of ice cream, Cody's phone vibrates on the table with a text message. He slides it open, reads it, and like a flame flickering out, his teasing grin fades from his face. There it is, that sullen look that he thinks he hides so well.

He doesn't answer the text.

"What's that?" I ask, nodding at his phone. "Ad for a hooker?"

"Ha ha," he says.

His phone vibrates again, and this time he shuts it off without looking at it.

"Seriously, though," I say, glancing at his phone. "What's going on?"

He pokes at his ice cream, before sighing. "My dad said another scout emailed about my visiting their team."

"Another?" I say. "I didn't know you had that many already. That's amazing."

Only he's not smiling.

"That is amazing, right?" I ask.

He doesn't answer.

"What? Having too many offers is stressing you out?" I can't imagine any other reason he would be upset.

He bites on his spoon and looks me right in my eyes, like he's trying to decide if he should tell me the truth. He seems to give it a lot of thought, which is more than I can say for myself.

"I'm going to hell if I say it out loud," he says.

I raise my eyebrows. "Did you kill someone?"

"No, but I'm sure you and everyone else I know will consider it on the same caliber." When I don't respond to his very ominous statement, he sighs and says, "I don't know if I want to play baseball in college."

There's a beat of silence as I take this in. "You mean

you want to go straight to the pros? What's so sinful about that?"

"No, I mean I don't know if I want to play at all after high school."

Oh.

Oh.

"But…" I have so many objections. So many questions. "But…"

Anyone who knows Cody knows that he's going to the major leagues. He's going to the frigging Hall of Fame. He's going down in history as one of the greatest pitchers in the entire existence of the sport. To think of him as anything but a legend of baseball is nearly impossible.

Which is why I can't wrap my head around what he's telling me.

"Why?" is all I can say.

He sighs and drops his spoon into his empty ice-cream bowl. "This injury has made me think a lot about playing ball," he says, glancing at the cast. "I've been so depressed and pissed about not being able to play, and I keep thinking about how one day I'm not going to be able to play. And not because of an injury, but because of age. I don't want to hit my peak and spend the rest of my life wallowing in self-pity and nostalgia. Or worse, be one of those athletes who keeps trying to come back and utterly fails.

I guess I don't want my whole life to be about baseball, and so far it has been." He lets out a frustrated groan. "But then, I feel bad about even thinking about turning down these colleges that want me to play. I mean, how many people would kill to not only go to college, but to go to college on a full-ride scholarship for doing something they love?"

I don't know what to say. I never expected this to come from Cody, who has, until now, had a one-track mind about baseball.

"Maybe it's stupid," he continues. He's still talking to me, but it's also like he's talking to himself. "But I've spent the last couple days trying to figure out what I like to do besides baseball. What if there's something else I like more than baseball? How would I know? What if I might be, like, a prodigal marine biologist or something?"

"But you love baseball."

"I can love more than one thing." He fiddles with his ice-cream spoon. "Don't you want to know if there's something else out there that you enjoy as much as pitching, maybe even more?"

I think about it, and slowly, I shake my head. "It's always been enough for me."

"Then maybe *you* should play professionally."

"Have you told anyone? Chizz? Your parents? *Joey?*"

Cody shakes his head, and part of me is like, *Awww, I'm his go-to confidante,* but the other part of me is like, *Well, shit. That means he trusts me to give him useful advice, of which I have none.*

"I think I'm having a mild identity crisis," he says, getting up to throw away his bowl. "I have to keep it on the down low."

I get up and ditch my empty bowl too. As we cross the terrace back toward home, I ask, "Is there something you were hoping I'd say to make you feel better?"

"Maybe that I'm not completely crazy."

"You forget who you're talking to."

He stops walking for a moment. He looks at me and smiles. Really smiles. Even though nothing has changed for him—he's still stuck in the same situation he was when we started the run—it's as if his way of dealing with it has changed. Not that I did much except listen to him, but maybe that's all he needed.

Under the lights, his brown eyes brighten, and my own eyes start drifting, from the glint in his iris, to the nearly invisible freckles on the bridge of his nose, to his lips, down his neck, and inevitably to the muscles on his arms.

And then to his cast.

"True," he says. "I would hope the girl who used to eat pickles with ice cream would not judge me for being crazy."

I shove him. "I was five."

He laughs, and we continue on our way. We talk about the most random things on our walk home—like how sea cucumbers puke up their guts as a defense mechanism against predators and how we saw a stray cat maul a bird when we were eight. We talk about unimportant things, because we're done talking about the important things. (Or, in my case, *avoiding* the important things.)

It's easy to talk to Cody, and when we talk like this, I realize how impossible it would be to be anything more with him. However much my hormones want to touch him all over, the ease we have with each other is too much to jeopardize. It's the age-old "dating ruins friendships" saying. But it came from somewhere—namely, the truth.

"Hey, remember in sixth grade I made a list of my least favorite people?" he says as we turn the corner onto our street.

"Yes, I do."

"I found it in some old junk I was sorting through in my room. Any guesses as to who was on the top of the list?"

"Probably me."

He smirks. "Yes, you were. But if it's any consolation, I've decided that you're no longer my least favorite person. Santino is."

My brain yells at me that this is another chance to tell

Cody about the wedding. *After he* just *said that Santino is his least favorite person? Yeah frigging right.* I shove all my sensibility aside and tease, "So now I'm your second least favorite person?"

"I suppose so," he says with a laugh.

We stop under a streetlamp in front of his house.

"You know," he says slowly, turning to face me. "You can always petition to be taken off the list." His gaze flickers down to my lips then back to my eyes. *Oh, hell.* Then he nonchalantly takes a step toward me, leaving less than a foot of space between us. One corner of his lips pulls up into a seductive grin. "Like maybe over dinner after the game tomorrow?"

Half my brain is like, *Oh, dear God. Be still, my beating heart.* The other half of my brain is like, *The game is* tomorrow?! *Already?!*

I push all thoughts of baseball from my mind and focus on this moment. On how I'm pretty sure Cody just *asked me out?* This evening he has given me multiple opportunities to divulge my secrets. To tell him about Santino. To tell him about the way he makes the pit of my stomach flip just by looking at me. All I have to do is say okay, and at least one of those secrets goes away.

But instead of letting myself be vulnerable, I narrow my eyes in teasing suspicion and go, "Are you asking me on a date?" It comes out jokingly, but inside my heart is pounding at the prospect of him saying yes.

"Marnie!" he scolds playfully. "I would never do something so preposterous!"

He delivers the line so smoothly that I can't tell if he was joking all along or he's hiding his disappointment at my response. But that's all it takes for us to destroy the moment. I hate him for backing down so easily. I hate myself for making it so easy for him to back down. I hate myself for lying to him about Santino and my true feelings, for offering no useful advice to him, and for liking him when it's so pointless and impossible.

"Guess I'll see you tomorrow then," he says, holding out his fist.

I halfheartedly return the fist bump.

"Sleep well, so you can kick the North Enders' asses tomorrow."

I nod, and he heads up his driveway without another word. I try not to watch him, his crazy-ass calf muscles, bare arms, disheveled hair, or fractured wrist. But I do anyway.

I'm almost compelled to call out after him. To tell him I'll take a rain check on dinner, to tell him us going on a date is not *that* preposterous.

But he opens his garage door and slips underneath

without a glance back at me, so I walk home. And all I can think about is how right Sara was. About how we both have two big, fat chicken hearts.

But maybe it's better that way. Maybe that's how my friendship with Cody has endured the chaos for so long.

13

SO HERE I AM, IN THE GIRLS' LOCKER ROOM, HALF AN
hour before the first pitch, staring at myself in a mirror.
It seems like a lifetime ago that I wore these gray softball
pants and a black-and-red jersey with *Corrington* scrawled
across the front in white and *Locke* printed across the back.
The last time I put on this outfit, I was preparing for my
softball regionals game. If I had known it would be my
downfall, I would've faked sick and let someone else shoulder the burden of pitching. Maybe we would have won.
Maybe I would still be playing softball. Maybe I wouldn't
feel like I'm about to *die* right now. How do I know I'm not
walking into my second pitching demise? Returning from
the ashes only to burn down again?

I take a deep breath and braid back my hair. Before that

last softball game, my mom braided my hair because my hands were trembling so hard. My hands are trembling now, but there's no one here but me.

I asked Mom this morning if she was going to come to the game.

She was busy wearing her accountant hat, and without looking up from her desk, she said, "Mmm... I've got a lot of work to catch up on today." Then she glanced up briefly. "I'm sorry."

I could tell she was sorry, not because she was going to miss the game, but because she knew she was disappointing me.

"You used to come to my games," I reminded her.

She smiled sadly but didn't say anything. I know there is a difference between her *going* to the games and *liking* the games. She only used to go because Dad told her she should support me. He probably never wanted me to hear him tell her that, but I heard anyway. Kids always hear things they shouldn't. If I had to bet my measly life savings on it, I'd guess that now that I'm seventeen and get that my mom is not a sports person, she figures she doesn't need to go. She might not care about sports, but it would still be nice for her to be proud of me. I don't know if she is. Dad's always been proud enough for the both of them.

I wind the hair tie around the end of my braid once

157

more for good measure. I take another deep breath, wishing my heart wasn't beating a million miles an hour.

Across the hall, the guys are gathered in the boys' locker room. They're waiting for me.

As I head over for the infamous pregame speech, I'm in a dreamlike haze. My feet move on their own, carrying me down the hall. My fist knocks on the door like Chizz told me to, and when I hear someone shout, "NO ONE'S NAKED!" my hand pushes the door open, and then my feet take over again. They bring me to the bench in the center of the locker room where fourteen guys, plus Chizz, are assembled. All thirty eyes turn on me, and my eyes—braver than the rest of me—dare to meet their gazes.

Chizz offers me a smile and then launches into the obligatory pregame pep talk, but my mind retains only arbitrary pieces: be proud that you got to the sectionals, focus hard, trust one another, and most of all, the dreaded *have fun.*

Ha.

Fun.

Why the hell did I try out for this? Exactly what am I trying to prove here? And who exactly am I trying to prove it to? Is this an "F you" to Joey, for doubting me? To Ray, for being a complete douchebag? To Nick, for being the untouchably perfect big brother? To my mom, for my not being "girly" enough? To myself?

Before I know it, everyone's standing. The guys whoop loudly, practically leaping out of the locker room, getting pumped up. I'm the only one left on the bench.

"Look alive, Marnie," Chizz says, tapping me on the shoulder with his baseball cap before following the rest of the guys out to the field.

I shake my head to clear my thoughts. *Don't think too much*, my softball coach used to say. *Overthinking derails your focus.*

I get up, stretch my arms, and force myself to take one step after another until walking doesn't feel like a struggle anymore. Outside the locker room, Cody is waiting for me.

He looks at me expectantly.

"No pep talks, please," I say.

He nods like he totally understands.

"Yo, Marnie," Davis says, slowing down so we can catch up. He waves a sheet of paper at me. "The lineup." I fall into step beside him as he runs his finger down the list. "We've played the North Enders a lot, so I'm pretty familiar with how they bat. Their coach always puts the light batters—you know, the guys who usually only hit singles—first and then follows them with his big batters."

That's a common strategy. I could have guessed that myself.

"This guy," Davis says, pointing at the fourth batter on the list—number twenty-eight, Harold Mathers. "He's a doozy."

"Doozy?" It sounds ominous.

"Think Ray, but on steroids."

My eyes widen, and I look to Cody for confirmation. He nods.

Well, shit.

As we approach the field, I scan the bleachers, wondering if Ray had the balls to show up despite his suspension from the team. Then I realize I don't care and stop looking.

Davis points to the back of the crowd. "See those four old, white dudes back there? Those are college scouts, all here to watch Mathers."

Damn. Four scouts for a junior at a small sort-of-out-of-the-way suburban high school. That takes some serious badass baseball skills, not unlike Cody's. Badass baseball skills that *I have to play against.*

We go into the dugout, and I stake a spot at the end of the bench, setting down my mitt and water bottle. Near the guest dugout, the North Enders team is stretching. I've spent a good amount of time with our baseball team, so you'd think I'd be prepared for all the buff, tough-guy looks. But when I see them all sneaking peeks at our team—or, mostly likely, *me*—I start freaking out again. They seem meaner. Stronger. So much testosterone should not be allowed in one place at one time.

"Marnie."

I force my attention away from our rivals. Joey stands in front of me.

"If you've come to give me a hard time," I say, "can you wait until *after* the game is over? And if you're going to curse me before the game starts, could you do it without me knowing? And also, in case you need a reminder, *we're on the same team.*"

I expect him to go, *Ha, ha, very funny*, and then proceed to give me a hard time anyway. But his face is stoic, which is highly unusual for Joey. "I just…" He starts hesitantly. I have never known Joey to be hesitant. "Have you talked to Sara?"

Sara? Should I be concerned? Before games, Joey can talk only about baseball and only think about what's happening on the field. That thoughts of Sara are even floating around in his brain right now is cause for suspicion.

"I always talk to Sara," I say.

"I mean, did you talk to her about…a thing…?"

"A thing…?"

"Never mind." He turns, but I jump in front of him.

"What thing?" I ask.

"The fact that you're asking means that she didn't talk to you about it, so…" He tries to move around me, but I step in his way again.

"What did you do?" Memories of yesterday morning fill

my mind. How Joey and Sara had made cryptic eye contact, and then he practically ran the other way.

"It doesn't matter," Joey says, avoiding my scrutinizing gaze. He picks up a nearby baseball and shoves it in my hand. "You should warm up." And then he hurries away from me.

I look at the ball in my hand then scan the bleachers by our dugout. Sara is sitting toward the top by my dad and Nick. She waves to me and smiles so widely that I can't imagine there's anything bothersome on her mind. Even earlier today, when I saw her in physics, at lunch… she seemed normal.

"Heads up, Locke!" Carrot shouts and attacks me from behind. "Don't look so down!"

I try shoving him away, but then he shakes my shoulders and yells, "Awaken, Beast of the Mound! Rise! Release thy fury on thine enemies!"

Laughter rises out of me, pushing away all other thoughts.

"Yooo," Jiro says, pulling us into a huddle. "Look who had the balls to show up." He points to the bleachers on the North Enders side.

It takes me only a second to spot Santino and Neha. They catch me staring. Thank God Santino has the brains not to wave. He holds Neha's hand down before she can give away our secret.

"What a dick," Carrot says, dropping his hands from my shoulders. "Injures our pitcher, still loses the game for his team, and then shows up to watch us. Bet he's mumbling voodoo spells under his breath."

"Should we tell Cody?" Jiro says. "Maybe they can duke it out."

"Yeah," Carrot agrees. "We all know *that* fight is overdue."

Jiro turns to me. "What say you, Marnie?"

"I say..." *What do I say? Definitely not the truth. Not right now.* "I say the best way to spite him is to win this game and move onto the semifinals."

Jiro claps me on the back. "Well said."

"In the meantime," Carrot tells me, "we better keep an extra eye on you. Can't lose another pitcher."

And then, sooner than I'm ready, the ump is giving me a baseball, the first North Enders batter is approaching the base, swinging his bat in a windmill-like motion, and Davis is crouching behind home plate, his mask pulled over his face.

A last-minute straggler from the North Enders team jogs across the infield to his dugout. He doesn't even attempt subtlety as he stares at me while passing the pitcher's mound. It's a loaded stare, intimidation mixed with curiosity. I'm sure they've heard they'll be facing a female pitcher, but still, I must be an anomaly to them.

The guy continues to stare me down, and though all

my instincts tell me to look away, to pretend I'm getting situated on the mound, I force my gaze to stay level with his. It's only when he finally turns away that I see what's printed on the back of his jersey: *Mathers.*

Number twenty-eight.

He joins his team in their dugout and starts whispering conspiratorially. Identical smirks grow on their faces as they all look at me and laugh. That can't be good.

Behind home plate, Davis gives me a slight reassuring nod.

My mind races. My heart pounds. I feel like I'm about to take a math test, like I'm sitting at my desk in the back of Mrs. Hollis's classroom, and she's coming down the aisle with the stack of papers, dropping an exam unceremoniously on each student's desk, getting closer and closer to me, when suddenly I can't remember anything I've learned.

The ump pulls on his mask and positions himself behind Davis. "Play ball!"

Not even a second passes before someone shouts, "You know they have a sport like this for girls! It's called softball!"

The comment comes from the fan section for North Enders.

I would not be surprised if they're here to shout obscenities at me rather than cheer on their team.

No matter, I tell myself.

"Come on, Marnie!" someone cheers.

And by someone, I mean Nick. And my dad. And Sara. They're in the bleachers together, watching me. Even if my mom isn't.

Stop it, Marnie. You don't have time to be bitter about it.

I roll my shoulders to loosen up. First things first— block out the spectators. I focus on Davis. He's giving me the sign for a curve ball.

I position the ball in my hand. If I can get this ball past the first batter, maybe the rest of the inning will turn out okay.

Deep breath. Good posture. Strong stride. And—

"Ball!" the ump calls.

Not exactly the way I hoped to get the ball past him.

Someone from the North Enders side whistles for me.

Ignore, ignore, ignore, I repeat.

Davis gives me another encouraging nod, but I already want out. I want out of this game, out this responsibility, out of this pressure.

But life only goes forward, and sometimes there's no way out but through.

Davis signals for a fastball.

I throw hard. The pitch breaks down and away from the batter. He swings.

"Strike!"

"DAMN STRAIGHT, MOFOS!" Sara yells from the bleachers behind our dugout. Chizz throws her a chastising look because she doesn't just say "MOFO." She says the full thing. But he gives me a satisfied nod.

I've thrown a strike on my second pitch. It's not an out, but it must be more than the North Enders were expecting. Both the team and their fan section have gotten abnormally quiet. The batter seems perplexed.

I'm not one to give weight to signs, but this seems like a good one.

———

By the bottom of the second inning, the score is still zero to zero. I'm on the bench next to Jiro, and we're watching Carrot bat.

We barely made it through the top of the second. At one point, North Enders had guys on first and third, and they almost scored, but Joey made a miraculous catch out in left field and finished the inning unscathed.

Luckily, our team's killer defense (and I guess the one strikeout I threw) curbed the North Ender team's will to be antagonistic. Sure, I can *feel* their disapproval, but at least they're not voicing their opinions out loud anymore.

There's a *clink!* on the field, and Carrot sprints to first, then to second. But that's as far as he gets, because then Brayden bats our last out, and I'm back on the mound.

I'm about to pitch to the first batter, when out of the corner of my eye, I spot Santino and Neha waving at me. It's almost like they're here to sabotage me, so I freak out that Cody and our entire team are going to see them and start a brawl.

"You got this, Marnie!" This from Cody, completely unaware that right across from him on the other side of the field is his archnemesis, also cheering for me, albeit incognito.

I'm so preoccupied worrying about the potential shit fest that I don't concentrate as well I should: my pitch lands straight on the sweet spot of the bat.

Number fifteen smacks the ball out between left and center, and as Joey scrambles to scoop up, the batter makes his way to second base.

The next batter gets a hit too, so now there's a guy on first and a guy on third. If they score, it will give the North Enders a reason to start throwing insults at me again. They've probably been hoarding them for when I screw up. Their time is approaching fast.

The next batter is the North Enders pitcher. He's got one hell of an arm, but according to both Chizz and Davis, he's a shoddy batter. As Davis instructed me before the start of the inning, I throw three wild pitches outside his strike zone, and he swings haphazardly at them all.

One down, two to go.

Unfortunately, the next batter is number twenty-eight, a.k.a. Harold Mathers, whose batting average has attracted those college scouts. Mathers is about seven feet tall, as wide as a refrigerator, and if he hits the ball, there will be no bucket large enough to catch my tears and those of my teammates. Because if he hits the ball, it's going over the fence. And if the ball sails over the fence, all three North Enders on the field will dance across home plate.

I would be buried alive for letting up a three-run homer.

I consider calling a time-out to tell Chizz that Jiro should pitch the rest of this inning—hell, the rest of this game—but *no*. I'm going to do this. I tried out. I got the part. I went to practice. All that effort won't be for nothing. Even if I screw up.

I throw a 12–6 curve—my pitch—and it takes all my self-control not to cringe as the ball sails toward Mathers.

There's an echoing *clink!*

Shit.

The ball shoots down the first baseline, and I pray it's going to be a foul, but it hits the line. Still in play.

Brayden, out in right field, scoops up the ball and throws it to first, stopping Mathers from going any farther. It's not as bad as a three-homer, but even so, they've scored a run.

The North Enders team and their supporters are loud in celebrating their point.

Suddenly I'm right back at softball regionals two years ago, reliving the last inning of that game. We're winning by one, and all I have to do is get the last batter out and keep the girls on second and third from scoring. I want to pull a Nick. I want to be the pitcher who keeps her cool even when the pressure is cranked to the max.

Instead, I do the opposite. I let up not one run, but two, all in one pitch. The game is over, and so are my days playing softball.

I shake myself out of it.

This is not that game.

I remind myself of what my old softball coach told me after that devastating loss: "It takes a team to win or lose a game. Not just the pitcher."

So I allow myself to take only partial responsibility for the North Enders scoring, and I do what you have to do in sports: forgive, forget, and move on, because the moment you start dwelling on the past is the moment you stop playing your best.

On the next pitch, we double play them, keeping the damage of this inning to one run.

The game slows to a golflike state, neither team scoring, neither team getting even *close* to scoring. Which, of course, means I'm doing my job well, but it also means the other team's pitcher is doing *his* job well too.

At the start of the fifth inning, Chizz asks if I want to let Jiro pitch. I've played more than half of the seven innings, but I tell him no because (1) I'm not that tired yet, and (2) I haven't brought out my submarine pitch.

So here we are.

Fifth inning.

Score: zero to one. We're losing. I'm pitching.

Time to try out my sidearm strategy.

Three batters. One of whom is Harold Mathers.

"You're slaying it," Chizz says. At least my success doesn't go completely unnoticed.

But I'm not the only one slaying it. In the next inning, the game finally propels forward when Joey smacks a ball over the fence, bringing in both himself and Carrot.

Score: two to one.

All I've got to do is keep the North Enders from scoring in the seventh and final inning.

It's the softball sectionals all over again. I'm sure everyone who knows me and what happened at that game is thinking it too.

"Should I go sidearm again?" I ask Chizz before going out to the field. "Or the usual?"

"I trust you and Davis to decide correctly."

"What kind of coach are you?" I scoff.

He laughs. "You know, sometimes what makes a pitcher great isn't their velocity or strength, but their instinct. Trust yourself."

So I go out on the field with nothing but trust.

Against the first batter, I throw two strikes with sidearm pitches. He hits the last pitch—a pop-up into left field. Joey catches it with ease. Out number one.

Second batter. First a foul. Then a swing and a miss. And then a fly ball right into Jiro's mitt at second base. Out number two.

Third batter. He hits the ball. Gets to second.

My heart drops to my stomach.

Fourth batter. The pitcher with the wild swings. I remember how easy it was to strike him out last time. He's probably expecting underhand pitches. So I decide to switch it up.

I throw overhand.

First pitch: right down the strike zone.

Second pitch: ball.

Third pitch: swing and a miss.

Fourth pitch: a hit—a foul.

Two strikes.

Davis gives me a sign with four fingers. A runner is taking a big lead off the plate.

The guy on second must be planning a Hail Mary steal to third. So I check him over my shoulder, and he takes a few steps back to second.

I turn back to face the batter. Davis flashes a four at me again.

I stand like I'm preparing to pitch, and then I whip around and throw the ball to Jiro at second base. The runner dives back, still safe, and Jiro throws the ball back to me.

Or rather, he feigns it.

Jiro watches as the runner stands and brushes off his hands. The runner's mistake? He steps off the base to do it.

Jiro moves his arm six inches to tag the oblivious North Enders player on the shoulder.

"HELL YEAH!" Jiro shouts with a triumphant jump, tossing the ball aside.

And that's how we win. With a frigging pick-off.

Because Jiro faked out a runner with a play that Little Leaguers use.

It takes a moment for everyone else to realize what's happened because no one but Jiro and I are celebrating.

Then, slowly, understanding sweeps the field, and all the guys run to dog pile on Jiro for his sneaky brilliance.

On the bleachers, my dad and Nick are screaming, but no one is louder than Sara.

Behind me, a chorus of "We Are the Champions" breaks out.

It's all so surreal to me—like I'm watching the game on TV and not actually a part of it. Chizz comes onto the field, smiling so wide that I wonder if this win has made him happier than seeing his daughter be born.

It happened so fast. First we were playing, and now the game is over. I look at the scoreboard to make sure it's real.

Two to one to Corrington.

Which means we're going to the semifinals. *We're going to the semifinals.*

In this fuzzy dream state, I look at the North Enders bleachers. Santino and Neha are on their feet. Neha catches my eye and gives me a thumbs-up. Santino delivers his congratulations with a slight nod, and then they disappear before anyone can catch on to them.

The next thing I know, I'm being lifted off the ground and spun in circles. The arm around my waist is strong but gentle, and when my feet find the earth again, I stumble back against Cody, whose good arm is still wrapped around me. I turn to face him, and he doesn't need to say anything to me—his smile says it all. A rush of adrenaline surges through me. *We won.* I pitched the entire game, and we *won.* We're going to the frigging semifinals! Cody is so close to me that I can feel him breathing against my body.

My nerves, drunk on victory, urge me to close the space between us. To give him the kiss that we both know we want. And I almost do.

But he makes the first move. Cody pulls me into another hug with his arm, lifting me off the ground.

"Fuck, Marnie," he says into my ear. "I'm so proud of you."

I pull away enough to look him straight on. "Thanks for giving me a push."

I think he's going to do it, going to kiss me, to really, actually kiss me, but then Joey and Jiro and a bunch of other guys stampede us with hugs and shouts and slaps on the back.

Chizz lines us up to do the good sportsmanship high-five routine with the North Enders team. I mumble my "good game" the way I was taught to back in Little League, but all I can think about is (a) we won, and we're going to the semifinals, (b) my mom wasn't here to root for me, but friggin' Santino Acardi was, and (c) I am so, so, so in over my head with Cody.

"Good game," I repeat, "good game."

14

AS IS TRADITION, VICTORY MEANS DINNER AT
Cecil's Grill House. The tradition may not be a big deal to
the team—they eat here all the time. All the waiters and
the manager know everyone by name. But for me, it's like
getting back on a bike when you haven't ridden for years.
I haven't hung out with a team since softball freshman
year. There are hardly ever more than four of us when I go
out: me, Sara, Joey, and Cody. Sometimes we're six when
Jiro and Carrot come too. But now, I'm part of this pack,
walking across Corrington Terrace with pride. Everyone's
talking over each other, being loud and obnoxious—exactly
as you'd expect from a bunch of high school jocks who have
just advanced in the postseason. They give no shits about
interrupting the couples on romantic dates who are sitting

at tables around the center fountain. Our team's excitement permeates every inch of the place.

As we approach the blue awning of Cecil's, I slowly regain memory of what it's like to be part of a team. I endured the athletic part of it, but the real test will be if I can last more than half an hour with the guys off the field, where there are no rules to follow or umps to referee or games to be won.

"Whoa, look at the crowd in there," Davis says, peeking through the front window of the restaurant. "Who wants to go in and get our name on the list?"

"Nose goes!" Carrot shouts, and immediately fingers fly to faces.

"Too slow," Joey says, jabbing Cody in the arm. "Go get our buzzer."

Clearly this is some sort of routine, because Cody doesn't argue. He pulls open the door and disappears into the crowd of waiting people. The rest of us wait outside where it's cooler.

"You're welcome to go with him," Carrot says, nudging my side. He gives me a knowing smirk.

The guys all look at me like they're in on the joke, waiting for me to cave into my pulsing heart. It's like they've all got stakes in some bet that I don't know about.

"I don't know what you're talking about," I say, even

though I know exactly what he's talking about. I won't give them the satisfaction, and just to prove it, I take a seat next to Jiro on a nearby bench.

"So," Davis says, "truth or dare. Marnie."

"Seriously?" I say.

"Team tradition. When we have to wait, we play Truth or Dare."

"Are you twelve?"

"Truth or dare, rookie, take your pick."

Wow. I changed my mind. I don't want to be part of their group if it means I have to regress to junior high behavior.

"Dare," I say.

"Go in there and make out with Cody," Davis says, smirking like a bitch.

I give him the finger.

"Fine, chicken. Then I dare you to make out with that guy over there," he says, pointing to a college-aged guy standing by the fountain.

As I contemplate if these are the kind of dares the guys always give, and how weird it would be for me to actually do it, the door to Cecil's opens, and Cody comes out with the buzzer in hand.

"I guess he's sorta hot," I say.

"Do it!" Davis and Carrot shout.

"Do what?" Cody asks. "Who's hot?"

"We dared Marnie to make out with that guy over there," Jiro informs him.

Cody looks at the guy then at me. Part of me wants to kiss the guy to see Cody's reaction. But then a girl comes out of a clothing store, walks up to the guy, wraps her arm around his waist, and kisses him on the mouth. Lovely.

"You were *this close* to getting me slapped in the face," I tell Davis.

He cackles in delight. "You lose this round, Locke. And here I thought you'd have some guts."

This goes on for some time. Brayden winds up throwing nearly three dollars worth of coins into the fountain. Joey asks a little girl if he can hug her stuffed penguin. Jiro confesses that he had a really inappropriate dream about the student teacher in his stats class. ("She's hot," Carrot tells us. "It's understandable.") Cody asks a passing couple if they've seen his pet llama strolling the area. (This is after he rejects the dare to have sex with me in the middle of the terrace. Thank God it's dark enough to hide the color in my face.)

We're *still* waiting for our buzzer to alert us that our table is ready when I get a text from an unknown number:

> Yoooo its santino, got your number from
> abram. Neha wants to take you out for

> a victory celebration (so do I, as another
> attempt to be a good cousin)

Trying not to look too skittish, I check to make sure that none of the guys are reading over my shoulder. I text back: im already celebrating with the team

> Gotcha. That's what I thought but neha
> insisted I ask anyway. I've gotta run a few
> errands for my mom while I'm in corrington,
> so text me when you're done. If I'm still here
> I can meet you back at your place

I check again to make sure no one's watching me too closely.

K, I send back.

I slide my phone in my pocket as Cody sits onto the bench next to me.

"Hey," he says. "I have to pick your brains about something."

"Go for it."

"Sara and Joey."

"What about Sara and Joey?" I ask, but I think I know where he's headed.

"Something happened between yesterday and today,

179

and I'm not sure what," he says. "But Joey is acting weird. I mean, weirder than he normally is."

"Hell if I know."

We both look over at Joey, who is sharing a video on his phone with the guys.

"Sara didn't say anything?" he asks.

"Nope. I've given up trying to pry details from her about Joey."

"I'm worried."

"About what? Sometimes they get like this. You know that. They'll go back to normal in a couple days, if not tomorrow."

The restaurant buzzer starts vibrating in his hands. Our table is ready. He stands and looks like he's got more to say, but he doesn't.

As we herd ourselves like hungry cows into the restaurant, Cody squeezes between me and Jiro. "You wouldn't *actually* have done it, right?" he asks, loud enough for only me to hear.

"Do what?"

"Make out with that guy."

I gain some satisfaction in knowing that he's still think-ing about that, even though it happened like twenty min-utes ago. I give him a sly grin. "You don't know me at all."

As we follow the host to the back of the restaurant, he says, "I know you would never make out with a random dude, but I also know you don't turn down dares so easily."

"Well, he *was* quite attractive."

He knows I'm teasing him, but still I feel jealousy radiating off him in the way he stiffens beside me.

"Don't worry. He's not as attractive as you," I say in an unmistakably joking manner as I patronizingly pat his stomach. I do this to disarm him because sometimes I can't help but flirt with him, especially when he makes it so easy. But when his firm abs flex in reaction to my touch, I mentally smack my forehead.

Touché, Cody. Touché.

We get to a giant circular booth in the corner, and I slide onto an edge seat next to Cody. We're sitting by a window that looks toward the fountain and across to the other side of the shopping center. The storefront displays are all lit up in a warm glow, including one for a dress shop. Which reminds me that I still have to get a dress for Abram and Geanna's wedding.

Mom hasn't gone helicopter parent on me in a few days, because I've hardly been home with school and baseball, but she'll be hovering over me soon enough. I suppose I could stop in to look at dresses after dinner. Maybe surprise her when I get home. Maybe that would make her resent me playing baseball a little less.

"Chizz said he'd pick up the tab," Joey announces after the waiter has left our table, which is cue for all of us to order the most expensive entrées on the menu.

Once we order (lamb chops for me—go big or go home, right?), Carrot decides to resume our game of Truth or Dare, much to my dismay.

"Joey, truth or dare?" Carrot says.

"Dare."

"Hit on the blond waitress when she walks over here."

"Veto," I say. "I refuse to take part in pigheaded activities."

"Fine," Carrot says. "Joey, I dare you to hit on Marnie."

Joey, who's sitting on the other side of Cody, rubs his hands together like he's plotting world domination, and then he leans over. Cody gives him the space, the bastard, and Joey takes my hand. "Do you have eleven protons?" he asks in an over-the-top smarmy voice. "'Cause you're sodium fine."

I yank my hand out of his, rolling my eyes, as the rest of the guys howl at his joke.

"Did you really use a science pun for a pickup line?" I ask, but I'm laughing too.

"Admit it. You're really turned on right now," Joey says, sitting up straight again. "Okay, Cody. Truth or dare."

"No, I will not make out with Marnie," Cody says, "and no, I will not tell you the last time I got a hard-on in school."

This peaks my interest greatly, but I keep my eyes fixed on the menu, already planning ahead for my dessert order.

"Fine, party pooper," Carrot says. "Let's play Penis instead."

"You're regretting coming to dinner now, aren't you?" Cody says to me.

"You have no idea."

Before anyone can shout *penis* over the rock-and-roll music playing in the background, our waiter comes back with our fried combo appetizers and drinks.

Luckily, I've grown up with a boy—and also with Cody and Joey (and Sara)—so I know how to secure food at a table full of guys. You don't wait to be polite. You take what you can get, and to anyone who misses out, it sucks to suck.

It's less of a free-for-all once our main dishes arrive because everyone has their own designated plates of food. The only things that are up for grabs from someone else's plate are the fries.

To be honest, I was worried I'd be the odd one out at this team bonding dinner, but they're actually all making an effort to make me feel like one of them. It's not so hard to fit in. And actually, it's really fun.

I forgot that being on a team isn't only about working well together on the field. It's about being friends and hanging out and just being silly together. I'm doing that with these guys, and they're letting me.

"You did say Chizz is paying for this little excursion, right?" Wes asks after all our stomachs have been defeated by Cecil's infamous large portions of food.

"Yes, I did," Joey says.

"Then methinks it's time for dessert," he says.

"Yes!" the guys cheer, and Carrot grabs the dessert menu from the center of the table.

Seriously? Dessert sounded good before we ate, but do these guys' stomachs have no bottoms?

I shake my head. "I'm sorry, but I don't think I could survive a dessert round." I grab my wristlet and my phone from the table and start to get up.

"You can't leave!" Jiro shouts.

"Yeah, what's so important that you can't stay and watch *us* eat dessert?" Carrot asks.

I gesture in the general direction of the exit. "I have to check out some stores for…" I think better of giving them an easy target. They'll give me shit for going dress shopping during bro-bonding night. "For some stuff," I finish.

"Some *stuff*?" Jiro says. "That's not vague at all."

"Is that code for tampons?" Joey asks.

I roll my eyes as the guys laugh like *tampons* is the funniest word they've ever heard.

"No," I tell them.

"Drugs?" Carrot asks.

"A male prostitute?" Davis says.

"A female prostitute?" Joey asks.

"Oh my God, you guys!" Just to make them shut up,

I say, "I'm getting a dress for this event I have to go to this weekend."

"A *dress*?!" Joey and Carrot cry.

"Yeah, a dress. In case you didn't realize, I'm a girl."

"*Whaaat?*" Joey says.

I stand up all the way. "Have a good night. I hope you all don't get kicked out of here before you get your dessert." Then I pull out a few bucks from my wristlet and drop it on the table. "For my share of the tip." I half salute them. "Good night."

"Nooo, don't goooo!" they call after me as I leave.

I know they're begging to be obnoxious, but still, it feels nice to be wanted, even if it's in the most ridiculous way possible.

I step out into the cool night. Now that the sun has completely set, the lights around the square seem more impressive. As I search for the least intimidating clothing store, I notice a sign hanging over an empty storefront. *CAMPO, coming soon.*

Campo.

Why does that sound so familiar?

That's right—Santino's mom is opening up a store in this shopping plaza. That must be it. The lights are on inside, but the door looks locked. I bet if the store were open, there'd be tons and tons of dresses for me to pick from. But if Geanna's designs are similar to her own clothing style, it'd probably be a real test for me to find something I'd like.

"Marnie!"

I turn to find Cody coming out of Cecil's.

"Where you headed?" he asks as he catches up to me.

I shrug. "Hopefully somewhere that won't make my bank account cry too much." I glance back at the restaurant. "You're not staying?"

"Nah. Hanging out with those guys when they're high on sugar is something a person should only do once in their life."

I laugh. "I can imagine. So are you going home?"

He slides his good hand into the pocket of his jeans. "Well, I thought if you wanted some company…"

"You wanna go dress shopping with me?" I arch my eyebrow. "Might as well stab yourself in the eye."

He laughs. "I'm sort of avoiding going home. My dad's grading tests tonight, which means he'll be cursing his students and wondering if he's really that bad of a teacher. I figured helping you try to find a dress would be slightly less painful than listening to that."

As usual my mind starts arguing with itself. One half is like, *Going dress shopping with Cody = mortification beyond belief.* The other half is all heart eyes, greedy for time alone with him.

"I guess you can come if you want," I tell him, sounding as indifferent as I can. "Just don't complain when your mind starts melting of boredom."

The first place we go is Samson's, the main department store. Cody and I head up the elevators to the juniors' section, and thus my hunt begins.

"Holy shit," Cody says when we get to the formal section, which has racks and racks of dresses arranged by color. "It's like a rainbow threw up here." He pulls a dress out of the lineup. "What is this color? Brown? Purple? It's like someone's shit after eating hundreds of grapes." Then he puts the dress back and grabs another hanger. "You should get this one."

He's holding a hot pink dress with a flamingo feather pattern on it.

"I think you would look very nice in this," he says, failing to maintain a straight face.

"Of course you would find this entertaining," I say, taking the dress out of his hands and hanging it back up.

I reluctantly peruse the racks, hardly even registering what's in front of me.

"What the hell?" Cody suddenly says. "A hundred and fifty dollars?" He holds up a shiny silver dress. "Why would you spend that much money when you could wrap yourself in aluminum foil?"

I laugh. "And now you understand the pain of dress shopping."

It takes him only five seconds to find another winner. "Can I see you try this on?" He holds up a white, nearly see-through tube dress that probably covers less than a bath towel.

"Hell no." I slap his hand away as he tries to pick out another hideous one. "You need to stop," I tell him, only half seriously. He's actually making this experience more interesting than it would be if I was alone.

"Can you try on one slutty dress?" he asks.

"No, pervert. Now quit fucking around."

"It's not like I haven't seen you half naked," he says. "Nothing will top the image I have of you in that black-and-red bikini you wore to the beach last summer."

A sensual spark rushes through my body as I remember how it felt having him check me out like twenty times when he saw me in that bikini. It was pretty much the most skin I've ever shown, and I'm not gonna lie, it was sort of exhilarating to completely stun him into submission for a good two minutes.

"If you're not going to try on a slutty dress, at least try on one of those poufy ones that's leaking sparkles," Cody says, pointing to a display on the far end of the dress section.

"I'm glad you're enjoying yourself," I say.

While he continues to amuse himself, I start down

another row of dresses. The problem isn't that I hate dresses. I think dresses are pretty and fun—when other people wear them. The painful part is how strange I feel wearing them. They only seem to call attention to what's wrong with me—my disproportionately long torso, my equally disproportionate long arms, and of course, my complete lack of cleavage. Not to mention, it's hard to find dresses when you're taller than the average girl. I always wind up showing more leg than I want.

Basically, for me, wearing a dress is like wearing the wrong skin. And to sit in the wrong skin for hours on end, even for just a day, is uncomfortable enough for me to have an aversion to the whole experience.

What can I say? I'm of the T-shirt and jeans camp. Down with your scratchy fabric and waist-squeezing devices of torture.

"Look," says Cody, who's been trailing behind me. I turn. "It's your favorite color." He pulls the dress off the rack and gives it to me.

It *is* my favorite color—a cross between maroon and burgundy. Clearly I must not be looking too carefully if I missed it on my way down the aisle.

I check the tag. It's my size. And on clearance.

"I still think you should reconsider the hot pink flamingo dress," he says.

"I think you should reconsider not talking."

But I keep the maroon dress to try on.

It takes me a whole half hour to peruse Samson's entire stock of dresses for junior girls, and in the end, I wind up with all of three potential winners. At the ten-minute mark, Cody's amusement with dress shopping ceased, and he decided to follow me around playing some word game on his phone. It looks difficult to play when he can use only one hand.

"I'm going to try these on," I tell him. "I won't be offended if I come out and you're gone."

"No worries," he says, taking a seat on a bench outside the dressing room. "I would never abandon you at a department store."

"Okay, good," I say, "so you can hold these for me." I give him my wristlet and my phone, and then I go in to the changing room to see how much damage these three suckers are gonna do on me.

Contestant number one: a simple knee-length black dress. I like it, but I know what Mom would say: "You can't wear black to a wedding! You're not *mourning* their marriage!" I could argue that it's not *all* black—there's a white diagonal band on the front. Not that any of this matters, because when I try it on, it's too loose on the top. It's made for people with boobs, so I have to nix it.

Contestant number two: a navy halter dress. The tag claims that it's knee-length, but I suppose they meant for someone shorter. The waist hits way above my belly button, and the so-called knee-length skirt hardly covers my upper thighs. The woes of being a tall person.

Which leaves contestant number three: the thin-strapped, maroon cocktail dress that Cody picked out. When I look in the mirror, I don't look like the same me, and I sure as hell don't feel like me, but it's closer than the other two dresses got. And it fits.

"Marnie," Cody calls from outside the dressing room.

"What?" I call back.

"Your mom is calling you."

I didn't tell her that I was going dress shopping tonight, but it's like she *knows*. I almost tell Cody to ignore the call, but then I think she might be calling to congratulate me. I'm sure Nick and Dad have told her about our win by now.

"Bring it here," I say.

"Uh, that's the *girls'* changing room?"

"There's nobody in here. Hurry, before she hangs up."

I can hear Cody's steps grow louder on the linoleum flooring. I slide my arms out of the dressing room and wave my hand for the phone.

"Are you not wearing clothes?" Cody asks as he puts the phone in my hand. I can hear the grin in his voice.

"No," I say. "I mean, no, I'm not *not* wearing clothes." I slide the phone inside the dressing room. It stops vibrating. Great. I try calling back, but the phone goes straight to voicemail. I text her and tell her that I'm dress shopping.

Cody knocks on the door again. "You're not going to let me see?"

"Get out," I say. "This is the *girls'* dressing room."

"Hypocrite."

I stare at myself in the mirror, contemplating. And then, with no warning whatsoever, delusional images of Cody coming in and getting all sorts of inappropriate flood my mind. Forget that Cody has a cast on his arm. In my mind, shirts come off. Skirts go up.

Stop it.

I mean, this *is* a very cozy space. And the entire fitting room *is* empty.

Right, like you want your first kiss with Cody—your first kiss ever—to be in the changing room of a department store. Real romantic.

Hell. What a place to have a romantic epiphany.

I want to kiss him.

Not just kiss him in the way that everyone expects us to—a one-time hookup where the entire relationship starts and ends with one kiss—but the *real* way. The way that means there will be more on the other side of the kiss. I want to *be* with him, and I feel that want so intensely that I can't remember the last time I've ever wanted anything so badly.

Admitting that to myself is scary and complicated and a relief all at the same time.

Without giving myself another second to change my mind, I throw open the door of the dressing room.

Cody's mouth drops open a bit. His gaze starts at my chest (even though there's hardly anything there), then trails down my legs, then back up to my eyes.

Normally I hate when guys get all horny and start checking me out, but when Cody does it, I feel good about myself. I like his attention. And I love disarming him when he least expects it.

"You look…" He swallows and then tries again. "You look…nice."

Suddenly I regret opening the door. What the hell was I thinking? I'm not ready for things to change. Don't get me wrong, I thoroughly enjoy being the object of Cody's affection, but I'm not prepared to cross the line if it means jeopardizing our friendship.

"Like…*really* nice," he continues.

Shit. My heart. It's going to explode.

One second of confidence has screwed me over.

I search my vocabulary for something, *anything* to say,

but I've got nothing. Of all the times to be speechless. I need to stay in control of the situation. If Cody makes the first move, God knows what he's going to do.

And then he does it. Cody steps inside the dressing room with me. He reaches out and pulls out the hair tie at the end of the braid. My breath catches in my throat as he starts undoing the braid, and my hair cascades over my shoulders.

His fingers trail from the ends of my hair, down my bare arm, sending spark after spark through my body. All I want is for Cody to shut the door behind him and for us to forget the reasons to be afraid of kissing one of your best friends.

My phone starts vibrating on the bench where I left it. *Dammit, Mom.*

Cody steps out of the dressing room abruptly. "I'll wait for you out there," he says, and then he disappears, just like that.

I close the door with a heavy sigh—out of relief or disappointment, I don't know.

I grab my phone, which turns out not to be a call from Mom, but a string of texts from Sara:

> You still chilling with the team?
> Is Joey there?
> Does he have his phone on?
> What are you guys doing?

You and Cody almost kissed on the field
after you won! I saw it! Don't deny it!
Can you ask Joey to open my texts?
I hope you're having fun. You deserve it.
Call me when you're done celebrating.

There's too much to process. What the hell is going on between Sara and Joey? I sit down on the bench in the dressing room and stare at myself in the mirror.

Holy shit, I almost made out with Cody.

I don't text Sara back. Instead, I try to decide what I want more: for Cody to come back in here or for me to go out there and for everything to be normal between us. Neither seems possible.

After a few minutes, I change out of the dress, pull on my skinny jeans and faded blue shirt, and braid my hair again. Hoping for the best, I head out and find Cody on the bench, his stare glued to his phone screen. It's like he never even moved.

"Ready?" he asks.

Okay. I can be chill. "Yeah."

He gets up and sticks his phone in his back pocket. I'm still holding the maroon dress, but I don't know if I want to buy it. Do I really want to think of that moment in the dressing room when I wear it to Abram and Geanna's wedding?

"So," he says, and I think, *This is it. He's going to say something about what just happened—about us,* but then he says, "Semifinals."

He regrets almost kissing me. He must.

"Yeah, semifinals," I say, playing along.

"Ready to kick more ass?"

"Perhaps."

"There is no *perhaps* when you go to the semifinals. There is only *fuck yes.*"

I laugh, grateful that we can slip into normalcy so easily. "Is that what Yoda would say if he was our age?"

"Yes, I believe so."

Then we both laugh, like we always do, and we walk with just enough space between us, like we always do, and I wonder how I could have lived all these years being okay with what we always do. I want more. I'm so wrapped up in my thoughts, I almost start toward the escalator.

"Hey, aren't you going to pay for that?" Cody asks, gesturing toward the dress.

Flustered, I nod and turn toward the line for the cash register.

Back outside on the terrace, our arms haphazardly brush against each other as we walk. I can't tell if we're walking closer on purpose, as if daring the other person to initiate the hand holding or if it's a coincidence.

"You think the guys are still there?" Cody asks, nodding at Cecil's as we pass.

"Probably," I say. "I bet they're on their second round of dessert by now."

"Dear God," Cody says. "I pray for everyone working there."

We keep walking.

His arm brushes mine.

Again.

And then again.

I can't focus on anything but how much I want to slip my hand into his, fold my fingers between his.

I'm so focused that I don't realize we're approaching Santino's mom's storefront until the chime sounds as the door opens and Santino steps out.

We all make eye contact. I look at Santino. Santino looks at Cody. Cody stares at Santino. We all stop.

Time freezes, and for a moment, I can foresee the apocalypse.

15

BESIDE ME, CODY TENSES. SANTINO'S EYES dart back and forth between me and Cody, and all I can think is, *Shit, shit, shit.*

Part of me thinks that Cody and I can resume walking, as if no one's there. But Santino gives me a slight nod and says, "Hi, Marnie."

Cody tears his gaze from Santino and looks at me. It seems impossible that we had that moment in the dressing room, because now he looks like he wants to stab someone with a pitchfork.

"Marnie." This is the unmistakable tone of Cody's voice that means: *Explain yourself RIGHT NOW.*

Santino bites his bottom lip. "So I gather you didn't tell him."

"Didn't tell me what?" Cody says, his stare still on me, his eyes sparking with anger.

It's like I'm underwater and can't tell up from down or left from right.

"Well…" Santino says. "Awkward."

"You know Marnie," Cody snaps at Santino when I don't reply. It's not a question.

"Of course I know Marnie," Santino says, his voice turning cold. I can't imagine he knows how to talk to Cody any other way.

"And *how* do you know Marnie?" Cody asks, his voice terse and strained.

The infamous Santino Acardi smirk appears. I know it—he won't be able to help rubbing our secret family union and pitching sessions in Cody's face. That asshole. If I don't interrupt, Santino is going to make a mess of everything. But it's like my tongue is gone. Vanished. When I need it most, it bails on me.

"Didn't Marnie tell you who helped her out with her sidearm pitching?" Santino asks.

Fuck him. *Fuck him.*

Fuck me.

Cody stalks off without even looking to me for confirmation.

"Cody!" I call after him. Halfway to the fountain, he

whirls around and opens his mouth to shout back. But he stops himself. Then he says, "You know what, never mind. I don't want to know." And then he turns and walks away.

Fury and confusion and hurt are written all across his face. It's like he's broken his other wrist, only this time, I'm the one who hit him.

This is the last thing I expected to happen tonight. After everything that went on between us, I'm stunned at how fast the tables have turned. I can't even get my feet to move. It's like I'm cemented here, and I can only watch him walk away from me.

"Marnie?"

I want to punch Santino. I want to break his wrist the way he broke Cody's. I can't believe I befriended that two-faced bastard. Did he really have to bring up the pitching like that?

"Marnie—"

I turn and shove him in the chest.

"Why'd you have to keep talking? Why couldn't you have kept your mouth shut?"

His eyes widen like he can't believe I'm mad at him.

"You did it to spite him," I say, practically spitting. "Why does everything have to be a freaking competition? Was it not enough that you benched him for the play-offs?"

"*What?!*" Santino cries. "This is *my* fault?!"

"Uh, yeah? Mr. *Didn't Marnie Tell You Who Taught Her How to Pitch?* Why the hell would you say that if not to piss him off? Why couldn't you just let us keep walking?"

He scoffs angrily. "Well, *sorry* if I don't let Cody decide when I can and can't say hi to my cousin."

"I'm not your cousin."

"You will be. And it's not my fault that you didn't tell him. You've had more than enough time. So no, none of this is my fault." He flips the keys in his hand around his finger. "Now excuse me. My mom left her phone at the store, and I have to get it home to her. And my *stepdad* is making pineapple turnover cake tonight. Wouldn't want to miss that." He pushes past me and then turns. "Oh yeah, congrats on winning your game and good luck at the semi-finals. I hope you don't fuck up."

Great.

Santino's pissed.

Cody's pissed.

But there's no question in my mind who gets priority. I hurry after Cody, calling his name, but he ignores me as he walks faster and faster, until finally I have to sprint to catch up with him. "Cody!"

He does an abrupt about-face to half shout, half plead to me, "Anyone but him, Marnie! Anyone in the *entire fucking universe* but him!" He stares straight in my eyes, the playfulness and mischief from earlier gone, replaced by pain and resentment.

Stupidly, I force out a lame, extremely guilty sounding, "It's not what it sounds like."

His eyebrows fly up in disbelief. "Really? *Really?* 'Cause it *really* sounded like you and Santino Acardi are *friends.*"

Okay, so maybe it is what it looks like.

"Are you going out with him?" he asks almost breathlessly, as if the words are burning him from the inside out.

"No! Cody, I would never!" He opens his mouth, most likely to object, but I interrupt before he can say anything. "My uncle is marrying his mom!"

This does nothing to soften his mood.

"That's what I have to get a dress for," I say, the desperation leaking from my voice. "My uncle and his mom's wedding. He's going to be my cousin, and I was trying to be friends with him to make my mom and my uncle and his mom happy. I was going to tell you. I really was—I really, really was. But I got scared you'd get mad. I should have told you. I was going to and—"

"YOOOO!"

Joey and the rest of the guys spill out of Cecil's, all high on their dessert.

"They're still here!" Carrot announces to the guys behind him.

Joey comes over, practically galloping from his sugar high.

"Waddup, friends?!" Joey shouts, hooking an arm around Cody's shoulders. Cody doesn't respond, and Joey draws back. "What's going on?" he asks, the smile falling from his face.

"Nothing," I say, as Cody turns to Joey and informs him, "Marnie's been hanging out with Santino."

All the guys hear. The biggest silence in history washes over us.

"You what?" Joey asks, glaring at me.

Great. All the points I've gained with the guys are gone. Just like that.

"Cody," I say, still more worried about him than anyone else.

"It's fine," he says, his voice quiet and tense. "Just go."

"But—"

"Don't worry about me," he says, but he won't meet my gaze. "Just go home. You're probably tired from pitching today."

He turns away, merging into the group of guys, using them as a shield against me.

Like hell I'll be able to sleep tonight. How will I, knowing he's pissed at me? I don't think he's ever been mad at me, at least not for real. Not like this.

The guys take Cody's cue and start walking away with

him, some of them shaking their heads in disappointment at me. Even Carrot and Jiro give me admonishing looks.

As they disappear out the exit of the town square, I sit on the edge of the fountain with my shopping bag at my feet, listening to the rush of water.

The guys hate me again, Santino and I are on piss-poor standings, and I'm way in the negatives with Cody.

Somehow, from where I started, I've taken two steps forward and about a hundred steps back.

16

WHEN I COME HOME FROM MY WIN-TURNED-loss night, I find Mom on the living room sofa reading the newspaper. At the sight of my Samson's shopping bag, she drops the paper and takes off her reading glasses.

"It took you long enough," she says with a smile. She gets up, holding out her hands for the bag. I give it to her, and she pulls out the dress.

"This is beautiful," she says. She holds it up against me. "Very nice." She kisses me on the head. "Thank you. I'm very happy you picked out a dress."

Well, actually, Cody picked it out.

Say, Mom, what would you do if you severely pissed off your best friend/the guy you might possibly have a huge, huge, huge, huge crush on?

Also, I really wish you would have come to the game. Are you going to congratulate me for winning?

"Are you okay?" she asks.

"I'm just tired," I say, putting the dress back in the bag. "I think I'm going to go to sleep."

Sleep, as in, lie in bed, stare at the ceiling, and drown in self-hatred and guilt. Cry.

Yes, I cry.

Not like sobbing with mucus dripping from my nose, but there are tears. My pillow gets wet. (I know, I know, I'm such an angsty teenager.)

Why didn't I tell Cody the moment I found out Santino was going to be my cousin? Was it because I didn't want to pile onto his shitty day, or because I thought he would be mad at me for something beyond my control?

When I put it that way, there is no argument. I'm an idiot.

And there it is, a fourth category of idiocy, and it's all my own.

I remind myself that our team won sectionals. We won, and *I* was pitching. Wasn't that what I wanted? Wasn't that why I threw myself headfirst onto the baseball team? Wasn't that why I put up with Ray's animosity, Joey's lack of support, and the seemingly unending pressure? I did it to win. To show myself I could.

And all I've done is show myself what an asshole I am.

How can something so good and so bad happen within hours of each other? I've reached a stalemate with myself, and I can't help but think that emotions are measured on a scale, where they cancel each other out until you don't feel anything at all.

―――――

Running sometimes helps me de-stress and sort out my feelings. I've been known to go on runs at midnight, like after finishing a ten-page paper the night before it's due. My mom is an advocate of sleeping off stress, but when I try to do that, my mind spirals into the depths of despair, where I spend hours tossing and turning in half-consciousness, thinking the worst thoughts my brain can possibly think.

So after an hour, I get up to run. I'll run until I'm so exhausted that I have no choice but to fall asleep upon impact with my pillow.

For the most part, our neighborhood is safe. Every once in a while, you'll hear of someone almost getting hit by a drunk driver, or in our case, someone stealing a bike from an open garage. But otherwise, it's safe to go running at night by yourself.

Still, though, I'd feel better if Cody was with me, not just because then we'd be on good terms, but because running around alone in the dark in a quiet neighborhood can get eerie sometimes.

As I round the corner back onto my street, a deep growl comes from someone's backyard. I flip so much shit that I almost run up Cody's driveway, ring his doorbell, and ask to borrow his baseball bat. (Or ask him to wrestle the damn wildebeest for me.) I know it's just Reilly Schwartz's devil dog, but still.

Of course, ringing Cody's doorbell at midnight—on *this* night in particular—would be a very bad idea.

But, bad idea or not, it doesn't matter, because as I pass his house, the garage door begins to open, and he starts dragging out the recycling bins.

He's three-fourths to the mailbox before he looks up and notices me. He stops where he is, and when our eyes meet, it's like an earthquake strikes me straight in the fault lines of my heart.

He drags the bins to the end of the driveway without acknowledging me, and he starts the hike back the way he came. There's so much tension filling the night air that I can't believe we haven't woken the whole neighborhood with our silence.

"So that's it. You're just going to ignore me?" I ask.

He stops and turns. "I don't have anything to say to you."

"Don't I get a chance to explain myself? Tell you the story?"

He comes back to meet me on the sidewalk. "I know the story," he says coldly. "First, Santino's going to become your cousin, and you don't tell me. And then you ask him to help you with pitching. And you don't tell me."

"I was going to."

"But you didn't."

"It...slipped my mind."

"Okay." He starts for his house again.

I reach for his arm to pull him back, but he shrugs out of my reach.

"Cody—"

Across the street, another garage door opens. It's Sara's garage, and from it comes Sara. And Joey.

"I *told* you it was them," Joey snaps at her.

Sara ignores him, and it's clear from the scowl on her face that Cody is not the only one who is extremely pissed off tonight.

"Great," I mutter. "Just great."

Without an invitation, the two of them cross the street to join us.

"So, traitor, come to beg for forgiveness?" Joey says to me as he aligns himself with Cody.

"Oh, get off your high horse, Joey," Sara snaps. "Like you have any right to come to *my* house in the middle of the night."

Cody rolls his eyes. "Fuck this. It's too late for this shit." And he tries to leave.

I jog after him, and this time, I grab hold of his wrist. Or rather, his cast. He flinches at my grasp, and I cower back.

"What?" he demands. "I don't feel like talking to you right now, okay?"

Suddenly, my regret turns to anger. "I'm trying to apologize! Can you let me do that? Can you stop hating Santino for five seconds and let me say that I'm sorry?"

He takes a furious step toward me so we're only inches apart. "I don't give a shit about Santino. This has nothing to do with how much I hate Santino. We've been friends forever, and you didn't even tell me you were hanging out with him. I told you about not wanting to play ball in college—something I haven't told anyone—because I trust you more than anyone else. I trusted you not to judge me, but apparently you don't trust me to do the same."

"Whoa," Joey says. "Whoa. Whoa. Whoa. Go back a second." He comes up the driveway to meet us. "Did I hear you right? Who said what about who not playing in college?"

I ignore him and say to Cody, almost spitting, "Can you blame me for being afraid you would be pissed at me for being friends with Santino? You don't hate anyone or anything, but you hate Santino, so how was I supposed to feel when I found out he was going to be my cousin? How was

I supposed to feel when he and his girlfriend were nice to me after all this time that you and Joey have been building him up as this monster?"

"Yeah, okay, no one wants to hear your excuses, traitor," Joey says dismissively. He points at Cody. "What was that about not playing ball in college?"

Cody, whose eyes have been fixed on me, now looks at his friend.

"You're quitting?" Joey asks again, his eyebrows furrowing in confusion and maybe also anger.

Cody closes his eyes and rubs them with the palm of his good hand. "Oh, fuck."

"What about all those hours you spent scouring the internet for info about D-one schools with me?" Joey demands. "What about all those camps we went to? What the fuck, man? How long have you been thinking about this?"

It's total scum of me to use their argument to my advantage, but I go, "Looks like I'm not the only one keeping secrets."

"Oh, shut up, Marnie," Cody snaps.

I step away and open my arms up like I'm addressing the whole world. "Well, excuse me if I'm the only one who's allowed to get shade for not sharing everything." I point at him. "You don't want to play ball in college." I look at

Joey and Sara. "You guys are fuck buddies or have been fuck buddies or have some big fat secret you won't tell us about." I gesture at Sara. "And you don't even want to go to college."

Joey and Cody both look at her. "*What?*"

"Hey!" Sara shouts at me. "You can't go dishing my personal shit just to feel better about your own!"

"Like this is news to any of you," I snap. "I'm a shitty person. I'm a shitty, shitty person."

"Don't throw yourself a pity party," Joey says. "You don't get a free pass for acknowledging that you're a shitty person. We're all shitty people. Cody puts on faces and pretends because he can't fucking talk about his emotions. You're friends with Santino. I cheated on Brie with *her*—" He points at Sara. "And then Sara fucking climbed the tree outside my window to fuck around *again.* Like five friggin' days in a row." He addresses her directly. "But I guess it's only okay when you do it, because when I climb *your* tree, then *I'm* the one who has to get a life."

No one says a word.

"So there," Joey says, his voice about to break. He stalks toward the street. "Good night."

I look at Sara, who avoids my stare and Cody's. She just shakes her head, suddenly very interested in her shoes. Is she crying? She walks back to her house without a word.

I can feel Cody's stare piercing my back as I watch Sara's garage close. I don't know how long we stand in this mess we've made.

Finally, after Joey has disappeared down the street, after all the lights in Sara's house have gone off, Cody says, "This doesn't change anything."

Frustration and rage course through me. "I said I was sorry!"

"Actually, no, you didn't. You aired out all our secrets, and then said you were a shitty person. I didn't hear an 'I'm sorry' in any of that."

I'm almost on the verge of tears, and I will them not to fall, at least not until I'm alone. "Then sorry! I fucked up! Okay?!" He opens his mouth, but I cut him off. "And I can be friends with whoever I want to be friends with. We don't have a binding contract that says we have to tell each other everything we do just because we've known each other for so long. I was going to tell you. I needed time. You can't possibly think I'd try and hide something that big from you forever."

"But you did try and hide it. You do know we see each other every day, right?"

"No, fuck you. You're not mad that I'm friends with Santino or that I kept it a secret from you. You're scared that one day I'll meet a guy who's not going to be my cousin and that our eleven years won't do shit to stop me from liking him instead of you."

That's it. Game over. I've struck his Achilles' heel. I don't even know if what I said was true or not.

His eyes are so cold they seem foreign to me. I half expect him to flip me off because I deserve that and so much more, but he disappears inside his house without a word.

I walk home slowly. I'm like a zombie as I trudge upstairs, change back into my pajamas, and collapse in my bed, still sweaty from my run and my fight. I stare at the ceiling.

I thought going for a run would help clear my mind. Instead, it made everything worse.

Much, much worse.

———

In second grade, we had this batty old teacher with gray hair named Mrs. Gianopoulos. Behind her back, we'd call her Mrs. Giant Octopus. The nickname was Joey's brainchild, and it stuck with us the entire year.

The year after Mrs. Giant Octopus taught our class, she retired. My dad says it was because she was seventy years old and probably wanted to spend with her grandchildren instead of other people's kids. But I know the truth. She retired because of us.

How do I know this? Well, on the first day of class, me, Joey, Cody, and Sara got into a fight over who got to sit in the comfy beanbag during silent reading time. It was a violent fight that ended with Sara pushing Joey into the bookshelf, which fell over and nearly smooshed this shrimpy little girl named Mia Sherman.

We were complete nightmares, all day, every day. I can't imagine how Mrs. Gianopoulos survived the whole year with us.

Thinking about this now makes me cringe with embarrassment and shame.

Thinking about a lot of things the four of us have done makes me cringe with shame. All our jokes and high jinks, all the random shit we've done out of sheer amusement or boredom, all the craziness we've gotten caught in together…

We were grade-A little rascals.

But I try to imagine what my life would be like if none of it ever happened, if we were boring kids with boring friendships who did boring things. If you take the three of them out of the equation, and I'm left with maybe half my life, and it's not particularly interesting.

I think about how we're still friends after all these years, the four of us, after all the silly arguments and stupid shenanigans, all the teasing and shoving and ridiculousness.

I don't know how we've made it this far. Will we endure after this? Will we be friends after this fight? I've taken for granted all they've done for me. How they've always been there for me, how they've made me *me*.

And what about after high school? We're nearing the end, nearing the time when we part ways to be adults. Can we stay friends if we're not hanging out on the sandlot every Saturday? How can friendships built off irresponsibility, immaturity, and pure child's play transcend into the adult world?

I don't know the answer, and it scares me that *this*—what's happened between me and Cody and what has caused one hell of a messy chain reaction—has marked the end of our childhood friendship.

It scares me because for the first time, I can see a future where the four of us do not exist together.

17

The last thing I want to do is go to a wedding. The second to last thing I want to do is put on a dress. The third to last thing I want to do is see Santino.

But alas, here I am, in a car on my way to a wedding, in a dress, where I will see Santino.

It's no doubt a beautiful day for a party—sunshine but no heat, a slight breeze but no wind. It's the kind of day that makes everyone feel good. You're dressed up, you're with your family, and you're on your way to celebrate one of the pivotal points of a person's life—their promise to spend the rest of their life with another person.

I feel so far away from all that. It might as well be storming, and we might as well be on our way to bury a corpse. Not to mention every time I pass a surface that is remotely reflective, I have to see myself in this dumb dress, which reminds me of Cody and how we went from nearly making out to not talking.

Friday in school was a nightmare. Cody, Sara, Joey, and I executed expert level moves to avoid each other all day. The classes we had together were so awkward even our teachers noticed.

"You two are quiet today," Mrs. Sorren remarked in English.

Cody shrugged. I kept my eyes focused on the pen in my hand.

During lunch, we all avoided the cafeteria. I know this because I went to the library to stay clear of them, and instead, I ran into all three of them in the most awkward meet up we've ever had. (Okay, so maybe we weren't so expert in avoiding each other.) Cody, quick-witted as he is, dodged into the computer lab, making it off limits to the rest of us. Sara took over our table in the atrium. And, I guess, realizing only one of us could stake claims to the cafeteria, Joey scurried away to the food and the rest of his friends, leaving me to find an empty corner under the staircase by the band wing, where I listened to the wind ensemble practice a John Williams movie medley for forty minutes.

And then there was baseball practice after school.

Dear God, that was a nightmare.

It was as if I didn't even exist. I would have rather taken devil eyes from Ray and snarky jabs about being a traitor from the team. But I got the cold shoulder instead. The silent treatment. Even Carrot and Jiro wouldn't look me in the eyes. The guys had finally accepted me, welcomed me into their brotherhood, and I botched it.

I hate how much of my life is out of my hands—the semifinals, Abram's wedding, and now everything with Cody. But that's life, right? It throws curve balls at you from out of left field, and you catch whatever comes your way, no matter how sucky a throw it is.

―――

Abram and Geanna's wedding reception is being held at this luxurious hotel ballroom. The enormous, dazzling chandelier that hangs above the dance floor belongs in a palace for kings and queens. They're really going all out, which makes me feel guilty for not being overjoyed to be here.

We're early, seeing as Mom—good sister that she is—offered to come by to help with the last details of the setup.

"You are abnormally silent," Nick says. We're sitting on a sofa outside the ballroom, ordered by Mom to stay out of the way. "You seem to be scheming. Trying to find a way to ditch the dress and find some shorts?"

"No."

"Plotting a coup on the kitchen staff to steal all the dessert?"

"No."

"Dude, what's wrong with you? Why are you being such a sour face?"

I shrug, which is so uncharacteristic that Nick stares at me like I've suddenly got five eyes and a horn growing out of my head.

"Are you still pissed that Abram's getting married to Santino Acardi's mom?" he asks. "I thought you were over that. In fact, I thought you were friends now."

"How did you know that you didn't want to play baseball in college?"

He cocks his head to side, apparently confused at this abrupt change in subject.

"Uh…" He rubs his hand absently over the stubble on his cheeks. "Well…it wasn't my entire life in high school. You remember how I was. I *liked* playing, but I definitely didn't dream about the Major Leagues." He bites his lip, hesitating before he says, "And you know, I don't want to be the asshole to break it to you, but getting on a Major League team might be *tiny* bit harder than getting on Chizz's team."

What exactly does it say about my life that he thinks I'm even *considering* the Major Leagues as an option?

"No, I'm not asking for me," I say, trying to ignore the image forming in my head of me standing on the mound at Wrigley Field.

"Who then?"

I shrug. "No one," I say. I can't even say Cody's name out loud, for fear it will break open the gate that's been keeping my guilt at bay.

"You used to be good at lying, you know."

I frown.

"Until you tell me, I'm going to assume that you're asking for yourself, and I just want you to be realistic about this. To play in college is hard. I know guys who are doing it, and sometimes it sucks. And for *you* to get on a guys' team, you're going to have fight real hard for it. Like spending all next year training and—"

"It's not for me."

He raises his eyebrows.

"Cody." His name feels like molten lead on my tongue. What is he doing right now? Cursing my name? Cursing Santino? Venting to Joey? Throwing darts at my photo? Inventing a time machine to go back to the day before we met to make sure it never happens?

"Why'd you say his name like that?" Nick asks.

"Like what?"

"Like he died?"

"I didn't."

"You did." He smirks. "*Oooo*, is Marnie finally having boy problems?"

"Shut up."

"That's what someone says when the other person is right."

"Shut up."

He leans back in the seat and crosses his arms smugly. "Well, well. Look who's getting all red."

I punch his shoulder, and he flinches.

"No need to be embarrassed," he says. "*Everyone* knows."

"Knows what?" I ask.

"Ha! *Knows what,* she says. Dad has already picked out which baseball players you and Cody should name your children after. Mom's been checking to see if birth control has been billed to our insurance. And *me*? Well. Older brothers just know these things."

I throw him a disgusted look.

"Don't glare at me like that. I'm right. I'm always right."

That he *is* right doesn't matter. The last person I want to talk to about boys with is my older brother. Sara is the one I need to talk to. Hell, I wouldn't even mind talking to Joey, because who else knows Cody like I do, maybe better? Certainly not Nick.

"I'm going outside," I say. "It's too hot in here."

"Is it because you're *in loooove*?"

I punch his shoulder again, and he topples onto his side laughing. I don't look back at him as I head into the ballroom where the hotel staff and members of the bridal party are frantically running around, yelling directions at whoever is listening. I give Geanna a halfhearted smile as I pass her, but she's trying to make sure there are enough chairs, so she doesn't notice.

The entire back wall of the ballroom is a floor-to-ceiling window, with double doors that lead to a patio overlooking a seemingly endless garden. I step out to take in the view and get some fresh air. There's a gazebo and a koi pond with a white bridge over it, which must be where a lot of brides take photos. About twenty feet from the koi pond are Santino and Neha. They're on a bench under a willow tree, and they're totally making out like it's nobody's business. Santino is in basketball shorts and a T-shirt—clearly not yet victim to his mother's demand to be dressed nicely—and Neha is in an aqua dress. It's completely disgusting, but I can't stop watching and wondering what it would be like to have someone you're so crazy in love with that you would make out with them without giving a damn about anything going around you—and at your mother's wedding reception nonetheless.

They're totally oblivious that they're being watched, but

after another few seconds of staring, I start to feel like a creep, so I silently do a U-turn to go back inside.

"Marnie!"

The *clickety-clack* of Neha's high heels echoes behind me, and it's impossible to pretend like I didn't hear, so I stop. Neha runs down the brick path with a giant smile on her face while she smooths the skirt of her dress.

Santino lags behind her, clearly disappointed at the interruption.

"I'm so glad you're here!" She gives me a light punch on the arm. "Congrats on your win the other day!"

"Thanks," I say.

"I also heard you and Santino are not on good terms right now," she says as he catches up.

I shake my head.

"We shall fix that." She grabs his hand and says, "Say you're sorry."

"*Me?*" he cries.

"Yes."

He pulls his hand out of her grasp. "What happened to being Switzerland? And who said it was *my* fault?"

"In my experience, it's always your fault."

I bite my lip to keep from laughing.

Neha stands besides me and links her arm around my elbow like we're best friends. Her energy and boldness is so intense it kind of overwhelms me. I suppose it would take such a person to be Santino Acardi's girlfriend. "I believe that this dispute involving you and Marnie and this Cody character, who I've heard so much about, stems from the fact that *you*"—she jabs a finger at Santino—"are too competitive. So say you're sorry for hurting her boyfriend—"

"He's not my boyfriend," I say.

"And for hurting your cousin in the process."

Santino's jaw drops. "Excuse me, were we not making out five seconds ago?" he asks, gesturing at the bench. "Have you no loyalties?"

Neha sticks up her chin. "Say you're sorry."

He points at the hotel ballroom. "Go inside."

Neha unlinks her arm from me and pouts at him. "Don't tell me what to do. Particularly when you know that I'm right."

He returns her pouty face and then pulls her in for kiss. "Can you *please* go inside? I promise to be good."

She smiles, and jealousy consumes me. Why can't I have this kind of relationship? How the hell does this happen? When there are literally seven billion people in the world, how do two people meet, become friends, and then become something *more* than friends, and *stay* something more than friends? How are they not paralyzed by the looming possibility that one day all that *something* might become *nothing*? I hate Santino, I hate Neha, I hate their adorkableness, and I hate that they're not afraid and that I'm so afraid.

Neha makes her way back inside, and I'm left with her despicable other half.

"Did you see the fish in the koi pond?" he asks.

I shake my head.

He starts walking toward it, and I follow, figuring this is his way of starting an apology. "There's this really ugly, fat one that looks like it's about to burst."

Water trickles down from the top of the rocky structure in a mini waterfall, and swimming in the clear pond are dozens of orange and white koi. On the side of the fountain is a small dish of fish food pellets with a sign underneath that says *Feed fish sparingly*, which clearly no one has bothered to adhere to. Santino points out the gigantic koi.

I watch as it lazily swims back and forth, pushing the other koi out of its way. It seems like there are too many fish in the pond. No space to move, no space to be alone. I wonder if koi mate for life.

And that's when I know I'm in deep—when I'm contemplating the romantic lives of a bunch of pudgy bug-eyed fish.

"So..." Santino says, watching the fish. "How's what's-his-face doing?"

I frown at him.

"Must still be mad at you."

I grab a handful of fish pellets and throw them in the water. All eight million of the fish swarm to get their share.

"I wouldn't dwell on it," Santino says.

And here I thought we were trying to come to a peaceful settlement. "I'm sorry," I say, "but I don't think I can take advice from you on this subject."

Santino bites his lip as if deliberating about saying what's on his mind. "I think you can, and I would actually advise you to do so. Because I think you've known Kinski so long that you've been desensitized to his arrogance and assholishness."

I drop the rest of the fish food I'm holding in the water and cross my arms. "You know, I thought maybe after all this—us becoming cousins, you helping me out with my pitching—you'd be less of a jerk."

"I'm just saying, if he can't put aside his pride to apologize for yelling at you and controlling who you get to be friends with, then he's not worth it."

A flash of fury burns through me. "Don't pretend you know shit about us. Don't you remember you said that our argument was *my* fault? Well, that hasn't changed. *I'm* the one who should apologize. *I'm* the one who's too chicken to do it. I've known Cody for eleven years. I've known you a week. And yeah, I think you're cool, and I think you're a good pitcher, but if you think for a second that you can turn me against him, then you really are as much of a blockhead as Joey says you are."

Santino tenses, his posture straightens, and he scowls. This is the Santino I've been expecting—the Santino who likes to give Cody hell, the Santino who's arrogant and cruel and likes to throw brushback pitches at other players simply because he can.

"Don't pretend you're the good guy here," I continue. "I haven't forgotten what you did to him. And to be honest, I don't know why I didn't punch you that night at the restaurant. God knows you would have deserved it for all the times you tried nailing Cody with a ninety-mile-per-hour pitch before you finally did." Santino glares at me as if Cody himself is confronting him. "Try all you want," I say, "but I won't let you convince me that Cody is anything else than what I've known him to be my entire life."

I give Santino a few seconds to refute, but when he doesn't say anything, I start back to the hotel.

Should I be concerned that I just torched what was left of the bridge between us? Did we ever even have a bridge to begin with?

Maybe. I don't know.

But all I can think about is how I wish I had recorded that conversation so I could send it to Cody and be like, "Hey, I just defended the shit out of you. Can we be cool now?"

But I didn't record it, so I do something really stupid.

I call him.

It rolls straight to his voicemail. For reasons that would take too long to explain, his voicemail message is Joey and Sara mooing for about thirty seconds. This gives me half a minute to decide whether or not I should leave a message, and if so, what to say.

By the time the mooing stops, I'm still too chicken. I hang up.

I spend the next half hour obsessively checking my phone, hoping that Cody will call or text me back.

He doesn't.

———

"Marnie! My favorite niece!" Abram plops down on the seat beside me. My stomach is now full of culinary masterpieces, and I'm ready to go home, but I'm the only one left at the table. Everyone else is either making a fool of themselves on the dance floor or making a fool of themselves at the open bar. Normally I'd join Nick in making fools of ourselves at the ice-cream bar, but I can't stop thinking about how mad Cody is at me. I can't even stop for ice cream.

"I'm your only niece," I remind Abram.

"'Tis true, my friend," he says. I'm pretty sure he's drunk, if not off of alcohol, then off of being a newlywed. "Why are you sitting all alone?" he asks. He points to the tipsy adults gathered at the side of the room. "Open bar." He points to the line of little children on the opposite side. "Open ice-cream bar." He nudges my arm. "Have some fun! You deserve it. I heard through the grapevine—meaning Santino—that you won the game yesterday. Celebrate!"

I give him a forced smile. "No thanks."

"*You?* Declining ice cream?" he says. "You're clearly not having fun. You should've invited someone to come with you. We gave your family a plus one just in case. Say, how 'bout a nice guy who could coax you onto the dance floor? Geanna's got some handsome relatives."

"Does she know that you can be an embarrassing dork sometimes?"

He pats my back. "One of my finer qualities." He leans his elbow on the table. "Now, come on, tell your old uncle what the problem is. He wants you to be happy, because he is happy, and because he's paying a lot of money for everyone to have fun tonight."

"I'm just tired."

"Liar, liar," he says. "I've noticed that you and Santino haven't talked much. I thought you guys were on good terms."

"*Were.*"

"He's your cousin now. Don't wanna start off on the bad foot."

I'd like nothing more than to tell Abram that his new wife's son is a jerk. But it's his wedding, and I don't think it's fair to start shitting all over it.

"Speaking of Santino, where is he?" Abram asks. We both scan the guests and spot him on the dance floor. He's slow dancing with Neha to a pounding Lady Gaga song.

They're swaying together on the side of the dance floor. Santino's wearing his suit, and Neha has given up on her heels. Santino whispers something in her ear, and she starts laughing so hard they have to stop dancing.

"Ah, yes," Abram says. "The most adorable teenage couple the world has ever seen."

It's hard to dispute that given the scene in front of me.

"I don't think princesses get treated better than she does."

Again, not hard to dispute.

"You know how he introduced me to her?" Abram asks. "He said, 'Abram, this is Neha, my bestest friend from here to the next galaxy. I'm going to marry her one day.'"

"*What?*"

"Yup. Exactly those words." He laughs, shaking his head.

So who is the real Santino? The guy who hits batters with ninety-mile-per-hour pitches? The guy who resents his mother for getting knocked up? The guy who treats his girlfriend like a goddess?

Maybe he's not just one of them but all of them.

"He's a pretty cool kid," Abram says, nodding toward Santino. "I couldn't have asked for a better stepson. You should really get to know him. He's a good guy." He stands up. "I hope you enjoy yourself at least a little bit tonight, Marnie. I'm off to slow dance with my new wife."

I nod and sigh. I want to enjoy myself too. "Hey, Abram?"

He pauses.

"If Geanna wasn't pregnant, would you still be getting married to her?"

He thinks about it for a moment. "I'd like to think so."

I don't know what to say to this, so I just nod. He pats me on the shoulder again and then maneuvers through the guests onto the dance floor to take Geanna's hand.

Even from here in my seat, the two of them look so happy together. What I wouldn't give for someone to explain to me at least a percentage of how love works.

———

At nine thirty, when I think everyone's getting too tired to continue, the party revives itself. First, three new flavors appear on the ice-cream bar, and then the DJ picks up the beat, bringing us out of the slow lull of rock ballads and into techno dance music, which inspires Santino's cousins to start a dance off.

When my parents start dancing to Taylor Swift, it's time for me to get some air. So I sneak back out to the garden, which is now lit up with ground lights and cute little gothic-esque lamps that seem like they belong in a fairy-tale village.

I make my way back to the koi pond, where the water is lit by red and blue lights. I grab a few more food pellets and start tossing them in, watching all the koi congregate for a bite.

"Hey."

Santino's tie is loosened, and he's undone the top two buttons of his dark blue shirt. At least he had fun after our fight.

"Hi," I say.

He looks at the koi. "I think you're going to make them all fat."

"They're already fat." I throw the rest of the food in my hand into the water.

Santino sits on the edge of the pond. "Look, I'm sorry for what I said about Cody."

The name sounds weird coming from his mouth, as if it's a struggle for him to say.

"I just…" Santino says, clenching his fists. "I just *hate* the guy."

"I'm not interested in hearing a rant about how much you hate him."

"I hate him 'cause I'm jealous of him," Santino says, which catches my attention. "He's just so fucking good, like…how can any seventeen-year-old pitch like that? *Eerghh*. He pisses me off *so much*."

This must mean the egotistical facade that he wears is a show. He has doubts about his talent. He knows he's not a god, as he would like us all to think.

"So you don't *actually* think he's an asshole?"

"Oh no, I do. I think he's arrogant as all get out. But that's neither here nor there." He picks up a fish pellet that fell on the stone next to him and tosses it into the water. "If I had known you were so in love with him, I wouldn't have said any of those things."

I swallow hard. "I'm not in love with him." People have got to stop throwing that word around so frivolously.

He gives me a semi-grin. "If that's the case, then you shouldn't talk so zealously about him. People might start thinking you are." He leans back on one hand. "So do you accept my apology?"

As far as I can tell, I don't have much choice. I shrug. "Sure."

"You know, it's a lot easier to forgive someone than it is to find the nerve to apologize."

"What do you mean?" I ask.

"I mean, you're afraid to apologize to Cody for lying to him, because you think he won't forgive you. But trust me, he wants to forgive you as much as you want to be forgiven. How hard was it for you to accept my apology?"

"Not that hard," I say. "But this is different. I don't really care that you insulted me or Cody. At least not as much as Cody cares that I completely betrayed his trust and our friendship."

Santino nods slowly. "Yeah, I guess." He looks over my shoulder and waves.

I turn and standing practically nose-to-window is Neha. She smiles at me and then makes a face at Santino.

"So that's your bestest friend, the one you're going to marry," I say.

"You talked to Abram. Though I won't deny it. She's my bestest friend, and as far as I can see, my soul mate for life."

"I honestly would never have expected you to be such a romantic goo pile."

Santino grins proudly. "There are lots of things about me that'd surprise you." He leans against the bridge railing. "So if you and Cody have known each other for so long, and you both have *a thing* for each other, why are you not, like, together?"

"How long were you friends with Neha before you started going out?"

He thinks about it. "Six years maybe?"

"Then shouldn't you know why we're not together?"

"Because you're afraid it'll ruin your friendship."

"Yeah."

"Sure, I get that," he says. "But then it got to the point when *not* going out was ruining our friendship."

"What do you mean?" I ask, only to realize a second later that I know exactly what he means.

"Whenever we were together, we danced around how we were both feeling, and eventually we stopped hanging out because we were afraid of what would happen between us."

"And then what?"

"Then I waited and waited, thinking that she would be the one to make the first move. Months went by, and nothing happened. We hardly talked to each other, and then one day, I went to her house and told her, 'This is stupid. Can we just make out already?' And then we made out."

Bullshit. That's too easy. "Is that *really* how it went down?"

"That is really how it went down."

"Wasn't that scary?"

"Sure. She was scared, and I was scared, and we

couldn't *both* be scared, or else nothing would ever happen. Someone's gotta give in."

The last person I'd ever expect to give me *relationship advice* is Santino Acardi.

And yet...

I look back at Neha, who is still standing at the window, now holding up a plate of cake.

Santino stands. "Cake part two. Good idea. I'm going to get some."

I nod but don't follow him.

"You're not coming?" he asks.

"Nah, I like it out here."

"Okay, whatever." He starts down the path but stops. "You know, my mom booked the place until one in the morning. She loves a good party. So there's still time to invite Cody if you want. I mean, if you get tired of being alone and watching everyone else have fun."

I narrow my eyes at him. "I would think you'd want Cody to suffer. Since you hate him and everything."

"Maybe. But you're my cousin. I want you to be happy, and I think you should have who you love."

Surprisingly, I don't feel the need to refute either of those statements.

"Was it worth it?" I ask.

He knows exactly what I'm talking about. "Sometimes

it is. Sometimes it isn't. Just look at what happened to my mom and my biological father. Do I think that was worth it? It terms of my life, of course. In terms of my mom's life, hell no. Her life was really hard after he left. How does anyone ever know if it's worth it?"

Santino's eyes land on Neha, who is still waiting for him inside.

"But," he says, "when it's worth it, it's *really worth it*. You know?"

I shrug. I don't know. How would I?

"It's like baseball," he says. "You play to win, and sometimes you lose, but that doesn't stop you from playing."

This I understand.

"Well," Santino says, "don't stay out here too long."

I watch him go inside. After a few moments, I follow in his tracks, but not to join the party. I need to find my family, I need to get home. Because it's late, and there's something I need to do tonight.

18

IT'S NEARLY ELEVEN O'CLOCK WHEN I STEP ONTO Cody's front porch. I hang out with his mom's potted plants for about ten minutes before I work up the courage to press the doorbell. A second too late, I realize I shouldn't have rung the doorbell in case his parents are sleeping, but I can't take it back.

A few moments later, Cody peels back the curtains of the bay window, probably to make sure I'm not an ax murderer. The look he gives me doesn't quite say *ax murderer*, but more *annoying salesperson*, so when he disappears from the window and the curtains fall back in place, I'm not entirely sure he's going to let me in.

But then the lock clicks, and the door swings open.

He stands there in all his six-foot, brown-haired, brown-eyed glory. He's wearing a red-and-white baseball henley and black basketball shorts. Nothing about him is any different than normal, but seeing him makes my stomach and heart and nerves all jittery.

Now I wish I'd kept on my dumb dress. I'd debated using it to seduce him into forgiveness, but it's not good to cut corners on an apology. There will be no stealing bases. I have to do this the right way. So I stuck with a pair of skinny jeans and a T-shirt.

"Hi," I say. *Good start, Marnie. A plus.*

"Hi," he says.

He stares at me so intensely I can almost convince myself that he's telepathically telling me to fling my arms around him so we can make out.

But that's likely wishful thinking.

"Sorry," I say, "it's late." Too bad apologizing for the time isn't as easy as apologizing for everything else.

He doesn't reply, but he steps outside and closes the door behind him. At least he's willing to hear what I have to say. Maybe Santino was right—maybe Cody has been waiting for me to do this.

He casually leans against the door, still silent. I have to make the first move. Hell if I know what that is, so I just start talking without thinking. Normally this gets me in trouble, but I didn't come with any more of a game plan (even if I should have).

"Cody, I don't know what to say, except that I'm sorry." *You liar, Marnie, there is* tons *more you can say.* I take a deep breath and let it out. Like I'm about to throw the first pitch of a game. But this is arguably much, much more nerve-racking. "I was going to tell you about Santino, about his mom marrying my uncle, and him helping me to pitch—I really was. I mean, at first I didn't because you were injured, which put you in a shitty mood, and I didn't want to make you feel worse. But then you were more yourself, and I was going to tell you, but…" Now here's the hard part. "But then I started talking to Santino and… I don't know. I sort of liked him. He's not so bad. I know it kills you to hear me say that, but…he kind of reminds me of you."

I expect Cody to deny this, to yell at me again, but he stays silent, his expression impossible to read.

"I mean, it was one thing for him to become my cousin—that was completely out of my control. But to like him? To want to be friends with him? I felt like I was betraying you—no, I *knew* I was betraying you. And I felt so bad. I didn't want to tell you because I was afraid you'd be pissed. I still should have told you. And I'm sorry that I accused you of being jealous. I know you were only mad because I lied to you. I'm sorry that Santino hit you with that pitch and now you can't play because you more than anyone deserve a chance to win the state title. And if I lose this for you on top of all the other stupid things I've done this week, it will make me the worst person ever. I'm really, really, really sorry. I'm a really shitty person, but I don't want you to be mad at me anymore."

I blow through all that in one breath. When I finish, I suck in a gulp of air. And I wait. And wait. And wait for a reaction from him. It seems like *eons* before he pushes himself away from the door and steps toward me. His look seems to have softened, making me want to run my hands through his tousled hair and kiss him.

Except I don't move.

He stares at me. "It's eleven o'clock."

"I know."

"You must be desperate."

Hark! I think I recognize that teasing deadpan tone and that small twitch at the corner of the lips, trying to hide a grin.

He's quiet for a while, and then he sighs, releasing the tension in his shoulders. "Well, lucky for you, so am I."

"You are?" The tension releases from my body as well.

"It's like physically impossible for me to stay mad at you, even when I really, really want to."

He runs his hand through his hair, mussing it up. He

sighs again, and then he sits down on the steps, inviting me to take a seat next to him. So I do—carefully calculating the exact spot that is not too close and not too far from him.

"Five-year-olds can hold a grudge longer than I can," Cody says. He hesitates, throwing me a half grin. That's all I need to know that we'll be okay. "And you're sort of adorable when you're sorry and self-deprecating."

Is he joking with me? Did I somehow manage to spew out a good apology in all that word vomit? Was it really that easy to fix this? And did he just call me adorable?

Cody continues, "I know that it's not *all* your fault."

"That's what I was *trying* to tell you."

"The being Santino's cousin part—not your fault. But the being a liar about it—that's all you." He looks down at his bare feet, his face falling into the shadows. "Still, I'm sorry that I yelled at you and that I didn't let you explain yourself before."

Wait. *He's* apologizing?

"But you have to admit, it was a lot to take in." He looks up at me and meets my eye. "You kind of blindsided me."

"I know. I'm sorry."

"I don't think that I'll ever like Santino, whether he's your cousin or not," Cody says. "But I don't want to be mad at you because he's your cousin…or because you're friends with him."

"Really?" I don't even try to hide the hope in my voice.

"You can be friends with whoever you want. I might not understand why you like him, but it's your choice."

The way he says all this, I can tell he's been thinking about it nonstop for the past two days. Guilt floods me as I realize how much turmoil this must have caused him—and how we could have avoided this if I had told him what was happening from the start.

"Anyway," he says, "I don't hate Santino nearly as much as I like you." He smiles at me—a real smile, and I'm thinking, *This is it. This has to be it.*

I lean toward him a bit.

"You know," Cody says, looking down, "you weren't completely wrong about me being jealous. In the thirty seconds before you told me he was going to be your cousin, I wanted to rip his frigging throat out."

My heart does a tiny flip in my chest. I hate how much I enjoy hearing that he was jealous. I also hate how much I enjoy the image of my best friend dismembering my new cousin. But alas, enjoy them I do.

"I wanted to come to you," Cody continues. "But I was scared." He laughs a little. "You can scare the hell out of me sometimes."

"I'm not scary."

"Not you per se, but the fact that I don't know really how you feel about me can be pretty unnerving."

He looks me straight in the eyes when he says this. Everyone else—Sara, Joey, Carrot, Jiro, even Santino frigging Acardi—seems to know how we feel about each other. How come we are the last to know?

"I've been trying to figure it out these past two days," he says. "And I finally realized that it's just been wishful thinking."

Wait…*what?*

"You were right. We have a *lot* of history, but that doesn't entitle me to anything more. And yeah, it hurts to think that someday you'll be with someone who's not me, but I can get over it." He glances at his casted wrist. "I got over this. I'll figure out how to move on." His eyes find mine again, and it almost hurts to hold his gaze.

Is this what he thinks? That I don't want him? *How? Why?*

"Cody…"

"I've always wanted something more," he says, "but I just need us to be friends, just like we've always been."

I can't breathe. I can't even feel my heart beating in my chest.

I want to protest, tell him he's wrong and needs to reconsider immediately, but before I can get a word out, he says, "It's better this way, right? Things are good the way they are."

I swallow hard. I want to cry, but I just stare at him.

"Marnie?"

A weak smile and a nod are all I can muster in response. *Shake it off, Marnie.*

It's not like I've lost him. If anything, we're sealing the bond of our friendship indefinitely. And how many people can say they're still best friends with their best friend from first grade?

So I do what I do best: I nudge him in the shoulder and joke, "So does this mean I'm officially off your list of least favorite people?"

He brushes a bug off my shoulder. "Marnie," he says with a small grin. "You've always been my favorite."

Hell.

How nice it would be to just kiss him senseless right now, but the equilibrium between us has been reestablished. He thinks this should make us feel better, but I feel so much worse.

19

WHEN I WALK INTO THE DOG SHELTER THE next morning before school, I expect Moose to greet me. He doesn't, and I'm disappointed. The place seems abnormally quiet. No yipping dogs. No Sara reprimanding the yipping dogs.

A volunteer behind the counter smiles at me. "Here for Sara?" she asks. Apparently my face isn't as foreign to the workers as theirs are to me.

I nod.

"She's in the back," the girl tells me.

"Thanks," I say and head through the door.

I peek into the kennel room. Some dogs perk up at the sight of me, but for the most part, they're quiet. Sara is not among them. So I move on to the small office next to the kennel room, where I find Sara seated at the desk, scrolling through a website on a computer that's about a decade old. Moose is sleeping by her feet.

"Hi," I say.

Sara looks up long enough to acknowledge that she heard me and then returns her focus to the screen. Perhaps she is less willing to forgive me than Cody.

It's a while before either of us says anything, then she finally goes, "So you're on an apology crusade?"

"I guess you could call it that…"

"I saw Cody this morning. He was happy." She says this all as matter-of-fact, like she's telling me that it's seventy-eight degrees outside and sunny.

I don't want to talk about Cody. I want to talk about her.

"I'm sorry I brought you into that mess on Friday," I say. Somehow saying sorry is easier now that I've had the practice with Cody. "I shouldn't have blurted out your problems."

"I know you shouldn't have," she says. Then she sighs and closes the browser, turning the chair to face me. "But it's done. It was a bad night to pick a fight with me anyway." She stands and stretches her arms over her head. Moose, always following her every move, gets on his feet too. "I wouldn't have gotten mad so easily if I hadn't already fought with mom and then had Joey show up unexpectedly."

I want to hear more about what's going on with her

college plans, with Joey. But I've already made a mess of things, so she can tell me when she's ready.

"I suppose I've got to air it all out now," she says, reading my mind.

I don't want to look too desperate for answers, so I just shrug.

Sara drops herself on the sofa against the wall, and Moose jumps up next to her. "Well…I guess Joey already announced that we were hooking up."

"Yeah, I got that," I say. "I just can't for the life of me figure out *why* or *when*."

"The why is easy—making out is fun."

Not that I would know.

"The *when* is the complicated part."

"He said he cheated on Brie with you. Which I find extremely difficult to believe."

"We were kinda drunk. Not that it changes how wrong it was."

Curiosity takes control of my tongue. "Can I get the whole story?"

"I suppose there's more on the table now than not."

I sit down in the spinny chair by the computer.

"So, last year, you remember how Brie and Joey went to winter formal, and you, me, and Cody went ice-skating? I came home dead tired and just wanted to sleep. But as I was about to crawl into bed, Joey rang the doorbell dressed up in his button-down shirt. So I asked him why he was there and not getting in Brie's pants. He looked all distraught, so I let him in. Mind you, my mom was out of town that weekend for a friend's funeral or something. So it was just me and the three dogs. And he told me that Brie told him at the dance that she's not sure she's straight, but she wanted to be with him until she figures herself out. So I asked him why he was telling me this, and he said it was 'cause he wants to ask me about sexuality and stuff because *I'm* not straight, and he wants to know what that's like and if maybe Brie could be bisexual and if that would mean they could still be together.

"So he was, like, freaking out, so I offered him some of my mom's wine to calm him down, and he was all for it. So I grabbed some glasses, and we sacked out on the living room floor. And I did my best to explain to him that there's no way for *me* to know who Brie's into, and that if she's not into guys like she thought she was, there's nothing he can do about it. Of course, after I did my best to console him, he was pretty shit-housed, and I was a *little* shit-housed, and he was cursing himself for falling in love with a lesbian who didn't love him back. And then, well, you know. Wine, no parents, sexual frustration…I don't know who started it. We keep blaming each other."

"So you just made out?"

"We did…stuff."

I raise my eyebrows at her.

"Stuff that involved no clothes and is too embarrassing to say out loud, so don't ask for details, because you won't get them."

I don't know what to say. Although I've had my suspicions, it still hits me hard. Sara and Joey. Hooking up and keeping it hidden from both me and Cody all this time.

"Do you *like* him?" I ask.

Sara leans backs and sighs. "Yeah, as a friend. But I wouldn't want to go out with him. It's all lust, to be honest. On both sides."

"You're sure he's not looking for more?"

"Trust me. He's made it very clear he's not. In fact, we both agreed that we were done for good. Until the other night when he came over and said he was bored, which is his code for 'Hey, let's have a drink and go to bed.' I put my foot down, and he got mad. But really, I think he was more mad at himself for succumbing to the temptation." She laughs a little. "We're a mess."

I'm not sure if she's talking about only her and Joey or all four of us. I suppose it's the inevitable mess that everyone has to muddle through on their way to adulthood. A rite of passage or whatever.

"Anyway." Sara gets up and grabs her backpack from the floor. "Shall we?"

I nod. "What about college?" I ask as we head out to my car.

"I told my mom I would look into some schools, and I have been, but the more I research, the more I don't want to go. The closest thing to a degree in professional dog loving is veterinary school, but I don't want to be a vet. I just want to take care of dogs and help them find homes." She gets into the passenger seat as I get into the driver side. "I'd rather work three shitty jobs in retail and stay home with my mom and the dogs than go into debt trying to get a degree that I don't want at some school that's hours or entire states away from here."

"And what does your mom say about all this?"

"She'll keep trying to convince me to get a degree. Maybe she'll succeed. Maybe she won't. I don't know. But my mom and I always find a way to make things work. We're quite the duo."

"Why haven't you talked about this before?" I ask as I turn onto the main street. I've always considered the two of us a dynamic duo as well, and I can't help wishing she felt she could confide in me about all of this.

"I don't know. We're always joking around, and I love that, don't get me wrong. But it's hard, not being able to laugh off problems like we're used to doing. Sometimes it's weird to imagine that we're almost adults with real life decisions to make. We're not innocent, little eight-year-olds anymore. Maybe it seems easier to pretend that we still are instead of recognizing that we have to deal with stuff—and that we've got the brains to really help each other."

She's put into words exactly how I've been feeling. Why it was so hard for me to confront Cody and Santino and to cope with a problem that involved more than someone violating the dib rule on the last chocolate chip cookie. Why it's so hard to admit what I actually feel about Cody, which I still can't seem to fully admit.

"So what are you going to do?" I ask her.

Sara shrugs. "I'm gonna go with my gut. Stick by my doggies. My mom has always been a good adapter. She's resistant when things don't go the way she wants at first, but she gets used to it way faster than she ever thinks she will."

Resilient Sara. Steadfast Sara.

She looks out the window. "Things are changing."

Things could mean anything, but I know exactly what she's talking about. "Yeah," I say, "they are."

She gives me a weak smile. "I guess we just keep playing."

I nod. "I guess so."

We're silent the rest of the drive. It could be any other day, me and her on our way to school.

But today, everything feels different.

20

THE SEMIFINALS ARE PLAYED ON NEUTRAL territory, which means I've got an hour-long bus ride to Armstrong High to dwell on what may or may not happen during this game against Charing East. It also means I have to spend sixty minutes in a vehicle with fourteen obnoxious guys, all buzzing with adrenaline and excitement, who are also slightly ticked at me.

My attempts to smuggle Sara on the bus failed (thank you, Chizz), so my only comfort are my headphones and a long playlist of pump-up music. I take a seat near the front. Not the front-front, because that's where Chizz is sitting, and I'm not in the mood to engage in conversation with him, so I take a seat about three rows behind him. This leaves a bunch of seats piled with baseball gear between me and the rest of the guys.

After we've been bumping along for a good fifteen minutes, someone starts calling my name. At first I think I'm imagining it, but then I hear it again:

"Lockster?! LOCKSTER?! LOCKSTER MONSTER, WAKE UP!"

I peek my head over the back of the seat. About half the team stares back at me, all with amused smirks on their faces. This throws me. Aren't they mad at me for betraying their brotherhood? Aren't they still shunning me?

"What are you doing all the way up there?" Carrot shouts as if we're miles and miles away.

"It's team bonding time, and you're not bonding with us!" Jiro shouts.

I find Cody's face among the bunch. He grins at me, and I know—he's given them the okay to stop hating me.

All of them are welcoming except Joey, who seems content maintaining the boycott against me, as evidenced by his focus on his phone screen rather than what's going on around him.

I lower myself back in my seat and turn up my music. I'm glad the team is willing to include me in their bonding time, but it doesn't feel right when Joey is still upset. I know—since when have I ever needed Joey's approval? But after hearing exactly what happened between him and Sara, I can't shake the feeling that I've labeled Joey as the immature pain in everyone's ass who is sometimes good for a laugh, while forgetting he's got his own stuff he's working through. I've spent my whole life thinking he's the one who unfairly begrudges me, but maybe *he's* been thinking the same thing, only the other way around.

Before I can start to regret all the annoying things I've done to him, whistling, cheering, and clapping break my thoughts. Cody drops himself in the empty space beside me, and Carrot shouts, "Get it!"

I pull out one earphone as Cody pulls a giant pack of Swedish Fish out of his pocket. "I have to open this up here," he says, "or else they'll attack me, and I won't get to eat any."

"They'd attack an injured person?"

"For these, they would."

I eye the candy greedily. "How do you know *I* won't attack you?"

"I'm willing to share with you." He holds the pack so I can take some.

I smile at him, and he smiles back. My heart cracks as I remember the night on his porch, how close we sat, how close I was to telling him how I really feel. But then I remind myself: I need to be grateful that we're friends. That we've been friends for this long and that we'll be friends for a long time to come. Never mind that I'll probably never get to know how good of a kisser he is. (He has to be a good kisser. Someone with a face like his can't be anything else.) At least we can share Swedish Fish and a seat on the bus.

As we munch, Cody asks if he can listen to my music, so I give him an earbud. And then I do the boldest thing I've done in recent memory—I rest my head on his shoulder, and stomach pleased with our snack, my mind consumed with the music, I sleep away the remaining miles.

———

It's clear from the start that Charing East has their shit together.

We get off our bus as they're getting off of theirs, but whereas we're loud and disorganized, they're disciplined and uniform. It's like their coach could be a drill sergeant instead of a high school baseball coach. Their team is matching in every way, from their blue-and-white team jackets to their caps to their duffel bags, right down to the way they walk.

None of them smile as they walk (or more accurately, march) off the bus.

"Why do they have to look like that?" I ask Cody.

"They're spawns of the devil," he says.

Jiro comes up next to me, his eyes following the

blue-and-white Parade of Death. "They've got the worst reputation in the state for playing dirty," Jiro whispers.

"That's encouraging," I say. "What are our odds?"

"We're pretty evenly matched," Cody says. "But like Jiro said, they're known for playing cheap, which will tip the scale in their favor."

"And by 'playing cheap,' you mean…"

"Their most infamous tactic is having their catcher make crude comments at the batter to make him lose focus."

"I'm pretty sure that's a page out of *The Sandlot*."

"Immature," Jiro says, "but effective. They're also fond of body checking."

"There's no such thing as body checking in baseball," I insist.

"There is when Charing East plays," Jiro says.

"Well, I'm a girl," I say. "They can't hit me."

"You better hope so," Jiro says.

At first I think he's joking, but he's not smiling.

As Charing East walks past us like drones, Joey shouts, "Left! Left! Left, right, left!"

Cody backhands his shoulder. "Dude, do you want to get your ass kicked?"

As he says this, a guy in the middle of the Charing East lineup looks back at us, trying to find the offender.

"Don't break formation!" Joey shouts at him.

"Dude, shut up," Carrot hisses, but there's a distinct laughter behind his words.

The Charing East team slows their pace, sizing us up. Their gazes end on me.

"Hot mascot," says a guy with really bushy eyebrows.

Cody tenses beside me. "Say that again, asshole."

Bushy Eyebrows stalks right up to us, towering over my head by at least four inches. If Harold Mathers was Ray on steroids, *this* guy is Harold Mathers plus Ray on *super* steroids. "I said, you've got a hot mascot," he restates emphatically, his eyes level with Cody's. "Where'd you pick her up? Walmart?"

The other team has now come to a standstill too, and I'm legitimately concerned that with all this testosterone in the air, a brawl will break out in next five seconds.

Before anyone starts throwing punches, I tell Bushy Eyebrows, "Your fly's open."

He looks down.

Just like that, our whole team busts up. They are that easy to entertain.

"Did you *really* fall for that?!" Joey shouts, doubled over in laughter.

Bushy Eyebrows narrows his eyes at me. Damn, he really *is* Ray and Harold's triplet. "Cute trick. Hope your pitching is as good as your insults."

He walks away, the rest of his team in tow. He must be their despot.

We all stand there for a moment, watching them settle into their dugout.

After a moment, Cody says to me, "'Your fly's open'? That's the best you could come up with?"

"Shut up."

He playfully bumps my shoulder with his as we make our way to our dugout. Normally I'd nudge him back, but any intent I have of joking around gets quashed when I catch Bushy Eyebrows watching us. Watching *me*.

This must be how Cody feels every time he's about to play a game against Santino.

21

DAD, NICK, SARA, AND EVEN SANTINO, NEHA, Abram, and Geanna are in the stands. I don't point this out to Cody, but I'm sure he notices anyway.

My mom isn't here. We had pretty much the same conversation as before the last game, but it escalated. She said she would try and come, but I knew she was only saying it. Instead of letting it be, I said, "You don't have to lie. Just say you don't want to go."

"Marnie, I said I would try and come, and I will try."

"Convenient. There's no way for me to know if you tried or not."

"Marnie, look at these stacks of papers," she said, her voice getting terse. "I'm days behind. I have phone calls to make, and I have to wait for these people to get off from their day jobs. I said I would try, so don't call me a liar."

"At least tell me straight up that you wish I wasn't such a tomboy and liked to get mani-pedis with you and wear dresses for no reason. You hate it. Just say it. You think I'm a total failure."

She rubbed her temples and closed her eyes. "I don't have time for this."

"You don't have time for *me*, you mean."

"Marnie!"

"I'm leaving. Bye."

I regretted what I said the moment I left her office. I hated how sarcastic I was, how angsty, how *teenager*. I know my mom is busy. I know she deals with bitchy clients all day. She doesn't need me to be one too.

All day at school, in between worrying about pitching, I kept wondering why I wanted my mom's approval so much about pitching—for a guys' team nonetheless. I wouldn't have thought I did. I've made peace with our many differences a long time ago. How could my subconscious have something so stupid buried inside it?

As I wave to Nick and Dad, I try not to let that the morning's argument work its way back under my skin. I try not to think that maybe if I hadn't been such an asshole, Mom would be here.

Armstrong High has a huge bleacher section for their baseball field, and it's a full house this evening. They wrap around the entire outfield, almost like a professional baseball stadium—but only one level and not nearly as many seats. And instead of a fence designating the end of the field, there's a concrete wall—also like the pros. They've got lush green mowed grass, comfortable dugouts with new benches, and humongous digital scoreboards above both dugouts. They even serve Chicago-style hot dogs at their concession stands—all the works sans the ketchup.

Might as well make this the home of the Cubs. No pressure.

"How you feeling?" Chizz asks me as I adjust my hair tie.

"Pretty good, actually."

He grins. "Let's make that *really fucking awesome*," he says, "and then we'll be in good shape." He hands me a baseball. "We're batting first, so you've got some time before you're on." He nods at the bullpen, which is also like a hotel suite compared to the one back home. "Get warmed up. Remember the other team is watching you closely, so don't show them your best moves."

I nod. Wrapping my fingers around the baseball triggers a rush of adrenaline.

Game time: T minus ten minutes.

Deep breath. In. Out.

Let's do this thing.

———

So it turns out the Charing East baseball team, in addition to being an intimidating and aggressive group, is also very good at playing baseball.

First of all, their pitcher is ambidextrous, and he frigging knows his shit. With one batter, he'll throw the first pitch with his right hand, then second with his left, and then the third again with his right. During warm-up, Davis lets it slip that their pitcher has been known to throw at speeds up to ninety-seven miles per hour. That is hardcore Major League shit that not even Santino or Cody could accomplish. (Okay, maybe Cody if he tried hard enough, but this Charing East guy does it like it's the easiest thing in the world.)

Second of all, Jiro was not wrong about their catcher getting mouthy behind the plate. According to our first four batters in the first inning, they all got some sort of insult thrown at them. Jiro says he was told a very vivid porn story.

It seems like only two seconds go by before the top of the first inning is over. Suddenly Chizz is patting me on the back, our team is pulling on their mitts and running to the outfield, and it's time for me to take the mound.

Cody squeezes my shoulder and gives me a baseball. "Knock 'em dead."

A smile is all I can manage.

No one vocally abuses me or tells me erotic stories while I'm on the pitcher's mound, but the hundreds of eyes on me, especially the dark pair belonging to the batter, are enough to freak me out. It dawns on me, *I am playing at semifinals*. One game away from state.

Dad, Nick, and Sara cheer for me, but they're the only ones. The bleachers are oddly quiet, our fans' doubt permeates the silence. Or maybe I'm projecting my own fears.

The batter is waiting. Davis shoots me the sign for a fastball.

Distinct snickers reach me from the Charing East dugout. When I make the mistake of glancing their way, Bushy Eyebrows, with a malicious smirk on his face, gives me a thumbs-up.

"Come on, Marnie!" It's Cody's voice of encouragement that drowns out the snickers. All his hard work—pitching practically every game this season and pitching five shutouts, including one no-hitter—and here I am, completely unfit to be taking his place.

I rack my brain for all the reassuring things people have

told me this week. The first that surfaces is about playing well and playing smart.

Keep your chin up, and soon enough, they'll see you've got a reason to.

I sure hope I have a reason to.

I shake these thoughts out of my head and position the ball in my hand. I stand up straight. I wind up, stride, throw…

"Strike!"

I let out my breath.

Maybe I do have a reason to.

———

By the end of the third inning, the score is still zero to zero, but not for lack of trying. There were close calls on both sides. At one point, our team had the bases loaded, but we failed to bring anyone home.

Charing East, realizing their offense isn't doing so hot, decides to up their defensive strategies by having their catcher amp up his level of asshole. Our team lets it go. We're too good to let that kind of immature behavior get to us, but then, in the top of the fourth, Joey loses his shit.

He's batting, and the pitcher is getting ready to throw when Joey suddenly steps away from the plate and shouts at the catcher. "I'll rip your throat out if you don't shut up, Lawrence!"

A five-minute holdup follows as both coaches, the ump, the catcher, and Joey hash out their argument behind home plate.

Since I'm not batting this game, I thankfully never have to experience whatever it is the catcher is saying to piss off all our batters, but after Joey manages to bring in one run, I have a feeling the Charing East team is going to up the ante.

In the bottom of the fourth, I strike out the first batter, who stomps off over the fact that he's been bested by a *girl*. The second batter hits a grounder to third base. Carrot scoops up the ball and throws it to Mitch at first base. What happens next happens so fast I barely even see it. All I know is there's a nasty collision, and Mitch and the batter are both knocked off their feet from the impact, sending them sprawling on the ground.

The batter gets to his feet. He looks unscathed. That might even be a smile on his face, the bastard. Mitch, however, is still on the ground.

Never have I seen a runner take a baseman out like that before—especially not in a high school game. It didn't look intentional, but after Jiro's warning about them playing cheap, I can't help but think it was.

Everyone waits expectantly as the first base ref talks to the ump. Chizz and a few other guys huddle around

Mitch. Everyone on our team seems ready to bury that runner in the sand.

A few moments later, Mitch is standing. He reclaims his position on first base, but whether he's actually uninjured or just too proud to take a seat on the bench, I can't tell.

I wait for the ump to call the batter out on interference, but instead the ump walks back behind home plate. Chizz starts shouting at him—I would be too—but the ump shakes his head: the collision was unintentional.

Unintentional, my ass.

But no amount of shouting will change this umpire's mind. The batter is safe. No penalty.

And the game continues.

Soon enough, it's clear that Mitch is not at 100 percent. His throws are a little off. And I can see him cringe at the slightest movement of his arm. The inning isn't even over before he decides to let Alec, a sophomore, take his place.

Charing East scores a run.

This only seems to encourage their foul play, because in the top of the fifth, the Charing East second baseman tags T. J. out by shoving his mitt into his trachea. T. J. doubles over, hacking.

"I tagged him out," the baseman says innocently. "It was an accident."

Again, the ump calls no obstruction. T. J. is out.

On my way to the mound after our three outs, Bushy Eyebrows—whose name I now know is Jonathon Prescott—passes me en route to his dugout. "Rough game today," he says. "Better watch out."

I'm not sure if this is considered a threat or not, so I file it under "Dumb Things Jocks Say."

I manage two strikeouts this inning, thanks to my sidearm tactics. As we planned, it throws the batters for a loop. I can't help but throw a *suck it* look at the second guy I strike out, mostly because he throws a hissy fit after the third strike, claiming it was *so not a strike, it was a ball!*

In a spare moment between batters, I give Santino a nod of thanks.

The fifth inning ends, and the sixth inning passes, and the score remains one to zero.

In the top of the seventh, Carrot exacts revenge on Charing East for injuring our players by belting a home run, tying the game one to one. If we were in the Major Leagues, we'd have two more innings for a comeback, but this is high school, and we only play to seven. We have to get this game into extra innings. Which means I've got three batters to keep at bay.

Three batters.

"Come on, Marnie!" Sara and Nick shout.

I shake my arms to loosen my tense muscles. I focus on my breathing.

I have been playing baseball since I was six years old. I've been taught by two of the best pitchers in the state.

I pitched at sectionals, and we won.

I've only allowed one run in seven innings.

I've made it this far without crashing and burning.

I might not be Cody or Nick or Santino, but I belong here—on the mound, mitt on my left hand, baseball in my right.

Davis throws me a sign for a changeup.

We get the first batter out on a fly ball.

The second batter is Prescott. I've been trying hard to strike him out all game, but so far, no such luck. This time, he hits a double. Which is about when I start having a mild panic attack. All I can think is, *You have one job to do, Marnie.*

One out.

Two more.

Two more.

The next batter, a tall, burly guy steps up to the plate. He takes a few practice swings and then winds the bat back over his shoulder. He shoots me a look like, *Give it your best, rookie.*

I take a deep breath as Davis flashes the sign for a curve ball.

I pitch, and I pray.

"Strike!"

I check Prescott at second. He's taking a big lead off, but when he sees me about to throw to Jiro, he returns to the base.

Another deep breath.

Davis gives me the sign for a fastball.

I pray and pray and pray. Then I pitch.

There's a *clink!* as the bat and ball make contact. I curse under my breath, but the ball lands in T. J.'s glove in center field. Prescott is going home.

T. J. makes an impressive throw all the way from center field to Davis, but it's a wild throw. Davis is stepping away, so I run to cover home plate. My heart is near to bursting as I leap to catch Davis's Hail Mary toss to me. The ball is in my mitt, and I make sure I'm not blocking the third baseline. All I have to do is tag Prescott before he reaches home. I'm expecting him to dive out of my reach, but instead, he completely *trucks* me.

He barrels into me like he's trying to break through a brick wall instead of a seventeen-year-old girl. He's a six-foot, two-hundred-pound guy, so there's no hope of holding on to the ball as I literally fly through the air. I never understood what it meant to have the wind knocked out of you—until now. I imagine this might be what a baseball feels like when it gets smacked with a bat.

I land hard on the ground and flip myself over.

Shouts of everything from curses to cheers ring out. Suddenly I'm shielded from the bright evening sun by people standing over me.

"Marnie," a frantic voice says.

Someone lets out a deep groan, and I realize it's me.

"Marnie, are you okay?" When I open my eyes, Cody is leaning over me. He gently pushes the loose strands of hair out of my face.

"Did we lose?" I manage to croak out.

"It's okay." Chizz. That's his voice.

But it is so not okay.

A blinding rage fills me. *This* is how we lost? If it had been any of the other guys guarding home plate, they could've taken the hit just fine, still holding on to the ball. Instead it was me—no catcher's gear, no body mass to match a guy like Prescott, no chance of enduring a blow like that.

In the end, it was because I'm a girl—lightweight and unable to stay on my feet.

"Is she okay?" I hear my dad shout.

It's his voice, the knowledge that I need to get up so he

doesn't have a panic attack of his own, that gives me the motivation and strength to get on my feet.

I sit up as Dad calls, "Marnie!" and he and Nick rush over.

"Careful," Chizz says. "She might have a concussion."

He starts asking me questions about how I feel, if I'm dizzy, if my vision is blurred, and so on. But all I can think about is how we lost. And it wasn't even because I'm a sucky pitcher. It was because I got blindsided on the very last play.

As I dwell on this, both teams line up for the good sportsmanship handshakes.

It sickens me that I have to do this, but that's how these things work. You're nice even when the other team doesn't deserve it. I stick myself at the end of the line behind Joey.

A couple of guys on the other team mumble, "Good game," as they half-heartedly high-five me. Then I get to Prescott at the end of the Charing East line. He squeezes my hand really hard and mumbles in a faux baby voice, loud enough for only me to hear, "Did the big, mean baseball player hurt your tiny ass?" He lets go of my hand and says in his normal deep voice, "Do yourself a favor and stick to being the mascot."

I just about punch him in the face right there, but out

of the corner of my eye, I see my dad and brother waiting for me.

I let Prescott have the last word.

I'll just pray extra hard that his team loses at state.

———

Turns out, I don't need to wait long for a reckoning.

As we're about to load the bus, Prescott and a couple of his buddies pass by. I hope they keep walking and let the hostilities of the evening die, but they stop, smirking like they've won the World Series.

"Always next year, right, fellas?" Prescott says. "And hey, some advice: putting a pretty girl on your team as a distraction is a cheap way to try and win a game." He smiles at me. "But, for the record, you are very pretty, and if you're ever lonely…" He gestures at himself. Then he winks and heads toward the Charing East bus with his friends.

"Fuck him," Carrot says.

I shake my head and start getting out the bus. But then I hear Cody go, "Joey, don't—"

I turn around and see Joey marching after Prescott. "Hey, douche face!"

For some reason, Prescott responds to this name. He turns around, and Joey's fist sinks right into his face.

"Oh my God, Joey!" a bunch of us shout, running over.

"Did the big, mean baseball player hurt your fucking face?" Joey shouts at Prescott, who's now kneeling on the ground, blood pouring out of his nose.

"Dude, get Coach!" one of Prescott's friends shouts. "Get him fucking expelled!"

"Don't!" Prescott commands as he puts pressure on his nose.

"Why?" his friend cries.

"Because he doesn't wanna admit that he got decked in the face 'cause he's a dumb ass," Joey answers.

Prescott glares at him through his bloodied hand, but it's clear that Joey is right.

As Prescott gets to his feet and storms away, his friends follow like ducklings. We retreat to our bus.

Chizz arrives moments too late, but he knows something's up. He asks Joey, who stays behind to…lie? Tell the truth? Who knows with him.

I watch out the window from my seat as Chizz starts going off on Joey. I can't hear what he's saying, but it's obvious his words are admonishing.

When Joey gets on the bus, I stare at him with awe.

"Keep your pants on," he says to me. "I didn't do it for you."

He goes to the back of the bus. Outside, Prescott, with

his nose pinched between two of his fingers, is getting tissues from their bus driver. Chizz comes toward our bus.

I look over the back of my seat. Joey is opening a bag of Doritos. He looks up, and our gazes meet.

All it takes is that one moment of eye contact to know that, yeah, he did it for me.

22

THE BUS RIDE BACK TO SCHOOL IS A SOMBER ONE.

We're all sitting bunched in the middle rows with none of the pregame excitement. All I want is to be home, in bed, making temporal distance from tonight. It feels like the bus ride from the softball sectionals two years ago. That was a shitty bus ride too. The sting of that loss hung around for months. Time is the only thing that will lessen the sting of this new loss.

I've got my head rested against the window, a quiet acoustic song playing into my ears, when Chizz slides into the empty seat next to me.

I lift my head.

He holds out his hand to me. Why would he want to shake my hand after we lost? Shouldn't he be turning that hand into a fist?

"Good job," he says as I hesitantly grip his hand.

"Maybe you don't really understand how baseball works," I say, pulling out my headphones, "but we lost."

He laughs. "Yes, we did."

"I'm sorry we lost."

He shakes his head. "Don't be sorry. Losing is a natural part of playing the game. There's nothing to be sorry for."

"I bet you wish you'd played a big guy instead of me."

"Marnie, the game could have easily gone the other way. If the ump had called interference when he should have, or if that huge foul that Joey hit had been a little to the left and became a home run, if T. J.'s throw to home had been a few degrees more accurate…"

"If anyone but me had been covering home."

"Beat yourself up over it if you want, but know that if I could go back, you would still be my first choice to pitch."

"You're just saying that."

"I'm not. I have no regrets about who I put on the field or how we played." He lowers his voice. "My only regret is that Joey didn't punch that little shit harder."

My eyes widen. Did he really just say that?

"Look," he says, "people were expecting you to fail. So you surpassed that by miles and miles. By light-years."

He gets up. "Believe me, Marnie, you've got nothing to kick yourself for." He starts for his seat at the front of the bus but then backtracks. "And," he says, "there's a spot on the team for you next year. If you want it."

I mull this over, taking in all that it means.

And I can't help but smile.

———

"Want a ride?"

I look up from my phone. My finger hovers over the call button, about to dial my dad to see where he is. He said he would meet me here at school to drive me home.

"Sure," I say, sending a text to tell Dad that Cody will give me a ride.

I follow Cody to his dad's car, which is parked in front of the school. Other guys are hitching rides together or getting picked up by their parents.

They wave to me as they leave, and I wave back. Joey passes, his duffel bag hanging off his left shoulder, and he punches Cody in the arm. He's about to punch me too, but then he stops, his fist suspended in midair like he can't figure out whether I'm allowed to get the bro-punch or not.

I decide to help him out. I make a fist and bump it against his, right into the knuckles that decked Prescott in the face.

Without another word, he continues on to his car. It's

then that I see someone is waiting for him—Sara. She's leaning against the trunk, phone in her hand. She looks up when Joey approaches, and Joey stops.

"Uh-oh," Cody whispers. The two of us, idiots that we are, stand there and watch.

Joey slowly goes to her, and Sara slides her phone into her back pocket. They start talking. I've never wished for supersonic hearing more than I do now.

"We should go," Cody says.

He doesn't move. I don't move.

They keep talking, neither of them smiling, but they're not shouting, either. If they were fighting, there'd be shouting. Neither of them know how to fight without shouting. Probably none of us do.

When they step closer, I gasp, thinking they're going to start kissing right here in the parking lot, but they just hug.

"Calm down, Marnie," Cody says. "Don't hyperventilate."

"Shut up."

Their hug doesn't last long, but the fact that they hugged at all is a step in the right direction. I mean, I know they've been way more intimate, but it seems…meaningful. Not the chaotic spontaneity Sara described.

"Is she going to get in his car?" Cody asks. "Place your bet."

"Shut up."

Joey goes around to the driver side of his car. Sara

doesn't get in. Instead, she goes to her car, parked a couple of spots down.

"Damn," Cody says.

"You think they'll ever tell us what they said?"

"Nope."

"Do you think they'll still hook up?"

"I don't know."

"Do you think they're together?"

"I don't know."

I punch his arm. "You're useless."

"Come on," Cody says, opening his passenger door for me. "Get in before I decide to leave you here."

I toss my bag over the seat and slide in.

We drive in comfortable silence, right up until he makes a left instead of a right where we're supposed to turn toward our houses.

"Whoa, where are we going?" I ask.

"Detour."

"Detour where?"

"A place."

"What kind of place?"

"A place with things you like."

And he is still completely useless.

There turns out to be Walker's.

He pulls into a parking spot right in front, and I say,

"What are we celebrating? Why do I have to keep reminding people that we lost?"

"Not everything is about baseball," he says. "We could be celebrating the end of school. Or the end of today. Or we could just be getting ice cream."

I almost say, *But that sounds like a date*, but I don't want to complicate the moment, so I follow him inside. The tables are empty except for one in the back, where a dad and daughter share an ice-cream sundae.

We take our ice cream to go this time—mint chocolate chip for him, coffee ice cream for me. He leads me across the terrace to the fountain. Which makes me think about the guy Davis dared me to make out with, the guy who was standing here with his girlfriend.

This is so totally a date.

Shut up, Marnie.

I sit down on the edge of the fountain, trying to (1) forget that this might be a date and (2) forget the entire semifinals game. But trying to forget something is the same as thinking about it.

"You are thinking really loud right now," Cody says, sitting next to me.

"I'm trying not to think about anything."

"Think about this." He pushes the cone in my hand so the top scoop almost smashes against my nose.

I shove his chest. "Dude, get away from me."

In retaliation, he scoots next to me, so there is literally no space between us. All the nerves in my body leap in excitement. I would not be surprised if the whole frigging world could hear them squealing, *Cody! Cody! IT'S CODY!*

I wonder what we look like, sitting side by side on the edge of the fountain. I'm in my sandy Corrington uniform, shirt untucked and unbuttoned, my hair falling out of its braid. I must look like a complete wreck. Me, the girl pitcher fallen from grace, next to Iron-Arm Kinski, in his jeans and faded red T-shirt, looking super normal but also devastatingly attractive.

We're together but not together. What a pair we are. What an odd friendship we have.

Cody eats the rest of his ice-cream cone, and then his phone buzzes. He looks at it and then says, "My dad wants me to let you know that he's sorry we lost, and he wished he could have seen you play."

"Oh…thanks," I say lamely. I think about my mom and how she didn't come to the game. Even if she couldn't make it, I wanted her to be proud of me, to congratulate me, to wish me luck. It would be nice to know she likes me for who I am, rather than being disappointed I'm not the perfect daughter she's always wanted.

"What's wrong?" he asks when I go quiet. "Besides the fact that we lost."

I sigh, and without thinking twice, I tell him about my mom.

"You are not a failure," he says. "Trust me. Losing one game doesn't make you a failure. And neither does not liking to shop for dresses, for that matter."

"I know. It would just be nice to know my mom likes me because I'm me, and not because she's obligated to as a parent."

"Don't be an idiot. Your mom loves you."

"I know," I say, and without thinking, I lean my head against his shoulder. The last play of the game keeps playing over and over in my mind. I can feel the bruises forming on my arm and hip where Prescott collided with me. I imagine if my mom had been there, she would've destroyed Prescott even more so than Joey. And it would have solidified her whole argument against sports. So was it better or worse that she wasn't there? Better that she didn't see me botch the entire game?

Cody puts his hand on my knee, and I'm in so much misery that I can't even respond.

"I know nothing I say will make the loss feel better," he says.

"I don't need to feel great. I just need to not feel this

sucky." I need to get this game behind me. Make it a distant, distant memory.

"It goes away," Cody says.

That's nothing I don't know. But waiting for it to go away will be agonizing.

His phone buzzes again. He reads the text with extreme intensity and sighs.

"What?" I ask.

He brushes the crumbs of his cone off his hands. "I'm playing on a summer team," he says. "And going to a camp where all these college coaches will be scouting."

Before, I would've been happy for him, but now that I know what's been on his mind, I'm not sure.

"Is that bad?" I ask.

"I don't know," he says. "I mean, I want to keep playing in high school, but…it feels like actively seeking out these college coaches and trying to impress them means that I'm going for it. And if I go for it, then I'm all in."

Cody sent videos to colleges and played on a summer team last year, but this is his junior year, which means he's entering the serious part of it. Honestly, I can't imagine him *not* playing baseball in college. I feel helpless giving him advice, the same way I did with Sara. Both of them make supporting me look so easy, and I can't seem to do the same for them.

"I think you should go for the pros," I say. "Then I can be like, 'Yeah, I know that guy.'"

He laughs. "That would be in, like, ten years."

"You don't think I'll still know you in ten years?"

"That's a long time from now," he says quietly.

"Hey, if in ten years, you're a pro pitcher or a marine biologist or a space cadet, I'll still be your number one fan."

I mean this in a joking way, but as soon as it comes out of my mouth, he looks down to hide the blood rushing to his face. We both know it's the absolute truth.

The truth is simple: I'm in love with him, and when I say that I'm cool with us just being friends, I'm lying. And when he says he can move on from his feelings for me, he's lying.

We are horrible, horrible liars, but that's not the crime. The crime is that we're both still too afraid to admit it.

A silence creeps between us. We're thinking the same thing. I know it. But neither of us voices the obvious. Instead, Cody stares at the hundreds of coins covering the bottom of the fountain, and I finish my ice cream.

I want to ask why he brought me here. Just to get me ice cream? To make me feel better? Because he's trying to take me out on a date without either of us saying it out loud? I can hear myself asking him. The words are on my tongue, and I repeat them over and over in my head, *Why did you bring me here?* But it's like there's cement holding my jaws shut.

I finish my cone. Cody stands and says, "Ready?"

I nod. "I'm gonna use the bathroom before we go," I tell him.

"I'll wait for you in the car," he says as I head back into Walker's.

On my way out of the bathroom, I pass the table with the dad and daughter, and the guy stops me. "I noticed your jersey," he says. "You wouldn't happen to be Marnie Locke, would you?" He points to my back, which has my last name.

Who is this man, and why does he know me?

"Uh…yeah…" I say. "I am."

He smiles. "My daughter Ling goes to school with you. She told me how you pitch for the boys' baseball team, how you're shaking up the school with your boldness."

"Oh…" I say, surprised that one of Joey's ex-girlfriend's *dads* knows about me.

"You guys celebrating a win?"

"No. Unfortunately."

"Too bad. I was rooting for you." He puts his hands on the young girl's shoulder. "My seven-year-old here, Xiao, was begging me to take her to the game after Ling told her about you. We couldn't make it, but look," he says to his daughter, "this is the girl who plays on the boys' baseball team." To me, he says, "She wanted to pick up a baseball the moment she heard about you."

What? I've been shaking up the school, *and* I've inspired a little innocent kid?

"Oh…" I wonder, if I could go back in time to tell my younger self how many days of my life I would spend at the sandlot, how many injuries I would get horsing around with the guys, how disappointed I would feel after losing the softball sectionals and then this semifinals game, what would I tell her? Would I tell her to pick a different hobby?

"Baseball is awesome," I tell Xiao. "Sign up for Little League."

And then I go, pushing out the door, the tiny bell overhead chiming behind me.

23

IT'S LATE WHEN I GET HOME. BUT MY MOM, who normally goes to bed at 9:00 p.m., is awake, sitting in the living room reading a book. No one needs to tell me she's waiting for me.

"Where were you?" she asks, setting the book down on the coffee table beside her.

"Getting drunk. Doing drugs. Running into traffic blindfolded."

"Marnie."

I sigh. "I was good. Don't worry."

"Dad said Cody was bringing you home. I didn't know it took an hour to drive from school to our house."

"We went to get ice cream."

She props her reading glasses on top of her head. "And you couldn't have told me that when I texted and called?"

"Moooomm." I flop facedown onto the sofa. I haven't even looked at my phone since I last texted Dad. "You don't have to worry about me *all the time*," I say, my voice muffled by the leather seat cushions.

She sighs, and the weight of the sofa shifts as she sits down by my feet. For a while she doesn't say anything, and I think maybe I've convinced her with my smothered whine of protest.

Then she goes, "Marnie, do you know how frightening it was for me every time you came home with bleeding, scraped-up kneecaps or a bloody nose or a broken finger? Sara or Cody or Joey would come ringing the doorbell, asking for you to play, and you'd run out the door, and I would never know if you'd come back in one piece or five."

I roll over onto my back and look at her. "Yeah, I know, Mama Bear wants to protect her child. I get it. But I wish you could have at least come to the game."

"And watch you get run over by a boy twice your weight? That was the first thing Nick told me when he got home." She squeezes my foot. "Marnie, I am glad that you have found something you're passionate about and that you've followed it through. But until you have your own child, you won't understand that, to me, nothing is worth you getting hurt." She sighs again, and I wonder if while I was at the game worrying about pitching, she was worrying about me getting hurt—which wouldn't have been uncalled for.

"Marnie," she continues, "I'm sorry you lost. And I'm sorry I didn't go to the game. And I'm sorry if you've felt like I don't care. I care very much."

I raise an eyebrow at her.

"Who do you think paid for all those tiny tot baseball camps? All the Little League gear? All the softball gear?" She pulls me upright by the hem of my jersey. "I'd hoped that by now it would be clear that we agree to disagree. But I still support you and whatever you want to do in life."

I lean in, and she puts her arm around me. "We can agree to disagree about baseball. I just want to know you aren't disappointed that I'm not more like you."

"Not disappointed," she says. "Never disappointed." She pats my shoulder. "Except maybe for the way you smell right now. Go take a shower."

I laugh. "Yes, ma'am." I get off the couch and undo my braid as I go upstairs, thinking that if I was the type of person who ran into traffic blindfolded for fun, Mom would totally be disappointed. Good thing I'm not.

Normally, I'm pretty good at getting in and out of the shower. It's a defense mechanism—if you take a quick shower, your mind doesn't have time to spiral into the abyss that is Shower Thoughts. There are scary things down there, and once you're mind has set up camp, it takes a whole lot of willpower and a shit ton of wasted water to get out.

Well, I'm totally intent on my usual in and out, so I can jump into my bed and fall into dreamless sleep, but then my stupid brain starts thinking about the game, the disappointment, and inevitably, Cody.

Damn you, brain.

I'm tired of thinking about him, tired of worrying about the next time I'll see him and if I'll be able to keep my cool.

Great, I'm thinking about Cody. In the shower. While I'm naked. Which makes me think about *him* naked in the shower—his nice toned body, tanned from all the time he spends outside running and playing baseball, his normally tousled hair, all wet, droplets of water rolling down his face and neck and chest and—

Shit.

Way to be appropriate, brain.

I shut off the water, even though there's still a little bit of shampoo left in my hair. I grab my towel and pull on my pajamas—a tank top and running shorts. As I blow-dry my hair, I focus on the whir of the hair dryer and nothing else.

When my nighttime routine is over, I dive into bed, pull up the covers, and slam my eyes shut. *Go to sleep, Marnie. Go to sleep.*

I'm exhausted and expect to fall asleep upon contact with my pillow. Instead, I find myself awake, staring at my ceiling at half past midnight.

This past week keeps playing in my mind—today's game, the practices, the wedding, first meeting Santino, Joey punching Prescott, even completely random things like one of the purple dresses I saw at Samson's but didn't try on.

It's one of those nights that my mind won't turn off. My brain lingers mostly on the game. It replays it all over and over, like I'm watching it in HD. The first pitch. The last pitch. Prescott hurdling toward home plate, ramming me like a bull.

Finally, the weight of sleep pulls on my eyes. *Thank you.*

I drift off to the "good game" high fives. The punch. The bus ride home. The talk with Chizz. Cody giving me a ride. Our detour. Ice cream. The fountain.

Cody.

Cody.

Cody.

I open my eyes again. *Dammit.*

When he dropped me off tonight, and we were sitting in his car in the dark, with only our garage lights to show me his face, I almost convinced myself to go for it, to screw the equilibrium. Because the equilibrium totally, totally sucks.

But then he said good night, and I said good night, and

I grabbed my bag from the back seat and got out, and that was that. He drove home, and I went inside.

My mind is so awake. How I can continually walk away from Cody and let him walk away from me when I know we both want to be together?

What was it Santino said? That we can't both be scared or nothing will ever happen?

I grab my phone from the nightstand. After getting blinded by the screen light, I blink and send a text.

Are you awake?

I wait and wait and wait.
My phone buzzes.

I am now, thank you.
Sandlot?

Ten seconds pass.
Then thirty.
Then a minute.
Then a minute and a half.
My phone buzzes again.

Okay.

Even though I live a couple of yards farther from the park than Cody, I get there first. I sit out in left field in my pajama shorts and tank top and listen to the quiet sounds of the breeze rustling the leaves as I wait. When five minutes pass, I wonder if he fell back asleep, but then I hear his footsteps in the grass.

My heart unexpectedly lurches at the sight of him walking toward me under the moonlight. This guy I've known since I was six. Who I have seen day after day. How can I have known him for so long and suddenly feel so different about him?

Or maybe this is what it is to finally allow myself to feel. Because sometimes your worst enemy is not your childhood nemesis or your sports rival, but yourself—your pride, your shame and fear and unrelenting belief that you are always right. Sometimes you need to give yourself a good mental kick and admit: I was wrong.

When Cody sits down next to me, every nerve in my body excites at the closeness of him, sending a shiver down my spine that I was wrong, wrong, wrong. Wrong to keep myself from him. Wrong to deny how much I want him. Wrong to deny him the truth of how I feel.

"You know, I'm perfectly happy hanging out during

normal hours of human activity," he says. "Just because you're an insomniac doesn't mean you have to try and convert me."

I find his light brown eyes. They're so bright and awake despite it being so late.

"So what's up?" he asks.

Like he doesn't know. He must know. After everything that has happened this week between us, he must know why I have brought him here, to this specific place, in the middle of the night.

When I don't say anything, he says, "Marnie, you're sort of freaking me out. Maybe you should see a doctor tomorrow in case you really did get a concussion."

"I don't have a concussion."

"Then are you okay?"

I nod.

He waits expectantly.

"I just…" I take a deep breath like I'm on the mound, ready to pitch another inning. "Can you close your eyes?"

"Yeah." He doesn't.

"Just do it."

"The last time you told me to close my eyes, I'm pretty sure you doused me with a hose."

"Does it look like I have a hose right now?"

He laughs. "Okay, okay." He closes his eyes. "Just don't do anything idiotic."

Define idiotic.

Gently, as if I might break him with a touch, I turn his chin toward me, and before he can open his eyes and ask what the hell I'm doing, I lean in and brush my lips against his.

His eyes fly open, but he doesn't move away. Our noses touch, barely, as he looks at me, his eyes burning with a question that I answer by kissing him again, deeper this time, fuller, unafraid. His whole body tenses, and I wonder if I've made a horrible mistake. But then he relaxes and responds with ease, sliding his uninjured arm around my waist and pulling me close.

He lies back, pulling me with him onto the grass. I settle on top of him, running my hand through his hair as I kiss him harder. I always knew we would be good at this. How could I have ever thought it could be any other way?

Cody runs his hand down my back and over my side, over the bruise from my collision with Prescott. I draw in a sharp breath.

He pulls away slightly. "Did I hurt you, or do you just get turned on really fast?"

"Maybe a little of both," I mumble against his mouth. "I have a bruise on my right hip."

He pushes us up into a sitting position and moves his hand away from my bruise as he kisses me, holding nothing back, his gentleness turning to hunger. He drags his lips to my jaw and down my neck. We have so much lost time to make up for.

I press myself against him, even though we can't get closer. He lets out a small moan, and I slide my hand under his shirt, dragging a finger down his stomach and over the button of his jeans.

He grabs my hand and withdraws his face from my neck.

"We are in the middle of a park," he breathes.

"The perks of choosing abnormal hours of human activity to make out." I lean in to kiss him again.

When I start pulling off his shirt, he stops me. "I don't think that's a good idea."

"I think it's a *great* idea."

He laughs quietly as he slides a finger against my jaw. "I have a fractured ulna. You have bruises and possibly a concussion. One wrong move, and we will both be screaming, and not in a good way."

I smile, resting my forehead against his.

"Another day," he whispers. "When I can use both my hands."

"I can think of plenty of things you can do with one hand. Or no hands, come to think of it."

"Shit, Marnie."

"It turns out I'm very attracted to you. I thought you should know."

He laughs again and kisses me one more time. Then we untangle ourselves from each other and lie back in the grass. I rest my head on his chest and drape my arm over his stomach. It's brand-new—all of this—but at the same time, it feels completely normal, like we've done it a million times. It makes me want to kick myself for being afraid of something that, in the end, wasn't scary at all.

"You know this is the first step down the path on which all friendships die, right?"

His hand slides into my hair. "Marnie, our friendship has endured way too much to ever die. It's made of Teflon." He kisses the side of my head. "We're invincible."

Invincible. I like the sound of that.

"What changed your mind?" he asks.

"I didn't change my mind. I moved a giant block of denial." Maybe one day I'll make him a list of all his qualities that make it impossible to just be friends, that made our daring leap unavoidable. It'll be a really long list to rival Dickens and Tolstoy and Hugo. His godlike skills on the baseball field, his sense of humor that is so compatible with mine, his perfectly crooked grin…

For a long while, we lie there in silence, maybe wondering if we're dreaming and if we will wake up in our own rooms at any second.

We're silent for so long, I check to see if he's fallen

asleep. But when I tilt my head, his eyes are open, and he's staring up at the sky.

"What are you thinking about?" I ask.

He smiles. "You. And today. And how this morning when I woke up I was thinking about what I'd eat for breakfast and how nervous I was for the team to play. The last thing I expected to happen was all of this."

I suppose I should take this as a romantic statement, but at the mention of the game, the crushing weight of disappointment falls on me again.

"What's wrong?"

I let go of him. "I'm sorry we lost."

He props himself up on his good arm. "Don't be sorry."

"Everyone keeps saying that. But I *am* sorry."

"It wasn't your fault."

"If you had been pitching, maybe we would have won."

"Yeah, maybe. But I wasn't pitching, and you were, and you played your best and kicked some serious ass—just like I knew you would. Who knows? Even if I had played, we still could have lost. Maybe in some other parallel universe we did win."

He's right, of course, but I so badly wish we could have won, even if it meant the stress of playing at state.

Cody reaches for my hand and squeezes it. "By the way, I heard what Chizz said about playing on the team next year."

I grin a little.

"Don't even think about it," he says. "I'm pitching next year. You can be my relief."

"If I decide to try out, I won't go easy on you."

"*You* go easy on *me*?" he says incredulously. "It's definitely the other way around."

I scoff. "Sure, okay. Whatever you say."

"Do we need to have a pitching contest? There's probably a ball we could fish out of the pond."

I sidle up to him and burrow my face in his shoulder. "You know what else I'm sorry for? I'm sorry that we had to wait this long for this to happen because I'm a stubborn-assed chicken."

"Marnie—"

"I mean, how many moments like this could we have already had if I wasn't such a dum-dum."

"Marnie, stop it," he says. "We were both chickens. It's both our faults. But I would not trade anything that has happened to get us here for a few extra kisses. All the stupid shit we've done, all our pointless arguments, all the nights we've spent together doing everything *but* kissing— that's what makes us *us*, and I wouldn't wish for anything different." He nudges my foot with his. "Would you?"

I lean over him. "I would…not." I slowly lift the hem of his shirt. "Here is a good place to be."

He pulls me closer and whispers against my lips, "Here is my favorite place."

And I tell him, though I'm sure he already knows, "Mine too."

ACKNOWLEDGMENTS

Sometimes I think about this book, and I am utterly in awe of how it is actually a thing. I started writing about Marnie when I was eleven. Back then, it was a never-ending plotless story about the silly things Marnie and her friends did. Every few years, I would revisit Marnie, rewrite the story from the beginning, and then forget about it without ever finishing. Until 2015, when Pitch Wars, hosted by Brenda Drake, came along, and it gave me that much-needed push to finish the story.

So I thank you, Brenda, and everyone else at Pitch Wars, for all you do for the online writing community. You motivate us and bring us together, and you are the starting point for so many writers' dreams, including mine.

You also introduced me to two amazing mentors,

Chelsea Bobulski and Lori Goldstein. YOU GUYS ROCK! You made this story 9,238,475,923 times better, and you helped me cross the bridge into this crazy world of publishing.

Thank you to this crazy world that includes the badass Courtney Miller-Callihan! I wish I could insert all my favorite thank-you GIFs here. I don't know how you do it, but you make things happen, and you always know the answer to *everything*. You are the BOMB DOT COM.

And thanks to Annette and everyone else at Sourcebooks for also making *Out of Left Field* 9,238,475,923 times better.

To the parental unit and siblings—I know you guys don't really understand why I'm always pounding at my keyboard, but you let me do it, and you let me be the weirdo that I am. Here is the product of that weirdness, so thanks for embracing it with me.

ABOUT THE AUTHOR

Kris Hui Lee is a contemporary YA author who also doubles as a graphic designer. When not writing or design-ing, she can be found cuddling with a doggo on the floor. Learn more at krishuilee.tumblr.com.